Formerly a teacher (last position: University of Pittsburgh, both English and Theatre Departments), until I simply could not face any more undergraduate papers—1977, I think. Or maybe '76. Also directed plays, reviewed books for the Pittsburgh *Press*, wrote catalog copy for a company that manufactures scientific instruments, and did a movie column for a now-defunct local magazine (absolutely *no* cause and effect there, if you please). Currently writing a column for *Mystery Scene* Magazine.

LIARS AND TYRANTS AND PEOPLE WHO TURN BLUE

BARBARA PAUL

LIBRARY OF CRIME CLASSICS®

MISTER E'S®

INTERNATIONAL POLYGONICS, LTD.
NEW YORK CITY

All of the characters in this book
are fictitious, and any resemblance
to actual persons, living or dead,
is purely coincidental.

Printed and manufactured in the
United States of America
First IPL printing October, 1991
10 9 8 7 6 5 4 3 2 1

Acknowledgments

Selection from *The Bald Soprano* reprinted from *Four Plays* by Eugène
Ionesco, translated by Donald M. Allen, copyright © 1958 by Grove Press.
Lines from "The Wanderer" reprinted from *Poems from the Old English*,
translated by Burton Raffel, copyright © 1960, 1964 by the University of
Nebraska Press. Excerpt from *Major Barbara* reprinted by permission of The
Society of Authors on behalf of the Bernard Shaw Estate. Lines from "The
Unknown Citizen" from W. H. Auden's *Another Time*, © 1940, 1968, Random
House, Inc.

CHAPTER 1

UNTERMENSCH

Eau de prison: jailhouse disinfectant, high on the we-recognize-it-but-wish-we-didn't scent parade. The room was hot, dark, stuffy, crowded. All that was needed was bars on the windows. And windows.

Splintery chair legs. "Should have worn trousers," Shelby muttered.

"Whassay, Miz Kent?"

"Nothing. Talking to myself."

One of the other men in the room threw her an uh-*huh* look. The man who'd spoken was Lieutenant Nicolosi—bushy head, beer belly, Certs breath. He'd hastily introduced the others crowded into the small room—"Shelby Kent, this here's mumble-mumble-mumble-Smith-and-mumble."

Smith and one of the mumbles had made little effort to hide their skepticism. Shelby shrugged mentally and dismissed them. She'd been to Pittsburgh at Nicolosi's request before; he knew what she could do.

"Okay, we're gonna bring 'im in now," Nicolosi said, and left.

Shelby and the five police investigators looked through the one-way glass into the interrogation room. The door opened and Nicolosi and an officer Shelby didn't know entered the room with a small, swaggering man—who, Shelby's now-practiced eye told her, was terrified. Drifter and grifter, incurably self-unemployed—the type was familiar. Pale, in his forties, trying to bluster his way out of a tight spot. The police thought he knew something about the death of a Pittsburgh-based jazz musician.

Nicolosi told the pale man to sit down and then stood directly behind him, literally breathing down his neck. The other officer sat across the table and started the questioning. "All right, Loser, tell us about Tuesday night. From the beginning."

It sounded like bully-language but wasn't. The pale man's name was Loos, so of course everyone called him Loser. So of course he was. "I already toldja." Loser couldn't decide whether to snarl or whine.

"Tell us again. What time did you see Wee Willie Bascomb on Tuesday?" (Shelby had seen photos of Wee Willie Bascomb; he'd weighed three hundred pounds if he weighed an ounce.)

"I toldja—around eight o'clock, at the Oyster House. His gig at the High Tone didn't start 'til ten."

"What were you doing at the Oyster House, Loser?"

"Same thing as Wee Willie. Eatin'."

"So you sat down at the table with him. Then what?"

"Then nothin'. We ate oysters."

"How long were you there?"

"I dunno. Half hour, mebbe more."

"Where was Willie when you left?"

"In the can."

"So you skipped out and left him to pay your bill. What did Willie talk about, Loser?"

"This, that. I don't remember."

Lieutenant Nicolosi spoke for the first time. "Remember."

Loser shot a nervous glance over his shoulder at Nicolosi. "Well, he was mouthin' off about that guy runnin' the High Tone. Said he wouldn't pay to have Willie's box tuned. Willie was gonna have to foot the bill himself, and he was shit-mad about it. That's the one you oughta be talkin' to—that guy what runs the High Tone. Willie sure was mad at him."

Nicolosi: "What was Willie pushing, Loser?"

Behind the one-way glass, Shelby Kent leaned forward in her chair.

"How do I know?" Loser said nervously. "I ain't seen Willie more'n two, three times since last summer. He coulda been clean, for all I know."

Shelby sat back in her chair. The policemen in the room were all looking at her, but she kept her face blank.

"Was it H, Loser?" Nicolosi persisted. "Coke?"

"I dunno, I tell ya!" The pale little man's voice went up a key. "I don't know what Wee Willie's been into!"

"Where'd he get the stuff? And don't tell me you don't know—you were Willie's beater back in the seventies." A beater was an errand-runner, a gofer. "You were dealing for him then and you're dealing for him now."

"You're crazy!" Loser shouted. "Back in the seventies—that was marijuana, man! Thassall! I don't know nothin' about the hard stuff!"

Both Nicolosi and the other officer snorted. Nicolosi decided to let it go for the time being. "What else did you talk about, Loser? Willie didn't sit there yakking about piano tuning for half an hour."

"Uh, uh, we talked about the oysters."

"What did Willie have to say about the oysters?"

"Uh, he liked 'em, uh."

"He liked 'em."

"Yeah, he liked 'em a lot." Loser warmed to his story. "He liked 'em so much he ordered another dozen."

"Was that before or after he slipped you the dope?" the other officer asked quickly.

Loser's face became even paler. "He didn't slip me no dope!"

"Then you slipped it to him. Which way was it?"

Loser swallowed noisily. "You're crazy. Nobody slipped nothin' to nobody."

"Sure, sure. Whose little beater are you now, Loser? Who sent you to meet Willie Tuesday night?"

"Nobody sent me! I met him by accident! I didn't know he was gonna be there."

Hmm, thought Shelby Kent.

Nicolosi was leaning against the wall, his eyes half shut, listening to the other officer hammering away at the Loser. When the little man was telling his story for the third time, Nicolosi straightened up and left the interrogation room.

Inside the observation room, Nicolosi closed the door behind him and said, "Well?"

Shelby cleared her throat. "He's telling the truth when he says he doesn't know anything about any drug operation. But he was lying when he said nothing changed hands at the Oyster House. And he lied when he said no one sent him to meet Willie Tuesday night."

"Aha," grinned Nicolosi. "Something *was* passed—I knew it! But it wasn't dope?"

"No," said Shelby.

Nicolosi nodded. "First thing you think of with musicians, I guess." He left and went back to the interrogation room.

The other officer was taking the Loser through his story a fourth time. Nicolosi listened a few minutes and then interrupted. "Loser," he said softly, "I'd like to believe you. I really would. I'd like to believe you aren't pushing the hard stuff."

"Swear to God, Lieutenant."

"But if we're going to believe you, you're going to have to tell us what *did* pass between you and Wee Willie."

"Nothin'! Nothin' passed!"

"Loser, we got two eyewitnesses willing to swear in court they saw something change hands at that table. Now don't tell me you and Willie was tradin' jelly beans. What passed?"

"Nothin'!"

"*Two witnesses,* Loser." The policeman was a better liar than his suspect.

The Loser was sweating now; his mouth worked soundlessly. "I don't know what it was. A package. Just a package."

"What was in the package?"

"I don't know! Swear to God! This guy, he give me twenty to—"

"What guy?"

"I don't know who he was—I never seen 'im before. He just come up to me and told me to take the package—"

"He just came up to you? Where?"

"On the street, man. Yeah, uh, Market Square."

"So this total stranger walks up to you on the street and hands you twenty dollars—to deliver a valuable package to Wee Willie Bascomb at the Oyster House."

"It wasn't like that—this guy knew I used to beat for Willie and—"

"Loser, Loser!" Nicolosi shook his head sadly and sat down next to the little man. "Don't you understand? You have to tell us the truth. All of it. What if there was PCP in that package? That means *you're* the one who'll be up on a narcotics charge."

"No," Loser squeaked. "He said it wasn't no drugs."

"Who said?"

"The guy that give me the package."

"Which guy is this? Who was he, Loser? Don't you see—there's only two people know what was in that package. Wee Willie and the guy that sent you to the Oyster House. And Willie's dead, Loser. He can't help you. *Somebody's* going inside—and it'll have to be either you or the other guy. Now who was he, Loser?"

Loser made a strangling sound and then gasped, "Mick Colley. It was Mick Colley give me the package."

The five policemen in the observation room were all staring at Shelby Kent. Shelby returned their look coolly. *First you thought I was a fake,* she thought, *and now you think I'm a freak. Up yours.*

Whoever Mick Colley was, he was well-known to the Pittsburgh police. In the flurry of activity that followed the Loser's announcement, Lieutenant Nicolosi managed to thank Shelby for her help and find a patrolman to drive her to the Greater Pittsburgh Airport.

Where, after stopping to buy a newspaper, the world's only living lie detector boarded a plane for New York.

CHAPTER 2

CHARON DRIVES SOUTH

One, two, buckle my shoo;
Three, four, je t'adore;
Five, six, pick up Styx;
Seven, eight, Latham Strait;
Nine, ten, whoyoucallingafathen?

Pittsburgh *Press*, front page:

TEGUCIGALPA (AP)—Fighting broke out yesterday near the remote village of San Pedro, Honduras, between armed insurrectionists and a contingent of United Nations peacekeeping forces stationed in Honduras.

Troops from the 44th UN Militia, stationed in Tegucigalpa under the command of Colonel Jean-Pierre Lefebvre, advanced to San Pedro in response to intelligence reports that arms and ammunition were being shipped secretly to the San Pedro area.

The fighting was intense but short-lived. After exchanging fire with UN forces for less than an hour, the surviving insurrectionists scattered throughout the jungle areas north and east of San Pedro. Casualty figures are not yet available.

Colonel Lefebvre said an investigation is being made to determine the source of the illegal arms shipments.

Editorial, page 8:

Honduras: No Hotbed of Rebellion

Yesterday's outburst of violence in the remote Central American village of San Pedro will be seen by many as a cause for alarm. Illegal arms and ammunition provided by unknown suppliers were turned against United Nations peacekeeping forces stationed in Honduras. Concerned persons may see a connection between yesterday's violence and a similar incident in Burma two months ago.

We have not had an international militia long enough for the peoples of this planet to feel full confidence in their newly formed global army. Its strength and stability have yet to be tested. Perhaps we are undergoing our first test now.

Not a test of military strength, but of moral courage. Uncertainty about an international military force can easily develop into paranoia if we allow ourselves to believe that opposition to the UN Militia is worldwide, organized, and dangerous.

This simply is not the case. There will always be pockets of political discontent in the world; this is a fact of human nature we have to live with. There will always be some who love rebellion for its own sake rather than for any social good it might ultimately accomplish—not to mention the personal gratifications rebels find in acts of defiance. Satan, remember, rebelled against God not because he thought the divine order was wrong but because he wanted to be Numero Uno.

What happened in Honduras was a knee-jerk reaction. And in Burma—two isolated incidents of nastiness. The danger lies not so much in the military threat such mini-uprisings pose, but in the psychological damage they can inflict.

Any big action provokes a reaction. The uniting of the world's military resources is one of the biggest single actions mankind has ever taken. We should have expected what happened in Honduras. And we shouldn't be too surprised if it happens again, in some other place at some other time.

Page 28:

MOBILE (AP)—Fifteen hundred defective World War II hand grenades were recently dumped into the Styx River in Alabama, according to Baldwin County Sheriff James Comer.

Recovery operations near the little town of Seminole, Alabama, began when two boys reported seeing a truck pull up to the bank of the Styx about midnight March 15. Sammy Turner and Billy Joe Welch said they were night fishing when four men began to unload large wooden crates from the truck and dump them into the river.

All the grenades examined were fitted with defective firing pins and were of the "pineapple" type issued by the U. S. Army during the Second World War. "Didn't know any of those were still around," Sheriff Comer commented.

The old-style metal casing of the pineapple grenade was scored to break into forty chunks of iron on detonation. After World War II the pineapple was replaced by the M-26 hand grenade, designed to throw hundreds of tiny fragments of wire.

Both types of hand-thrown fragmentation grenades are now obsolete. UN Militiamen are equipped with chemical grenades (incendiary and tear gas) and rifle-launched antitank grenades.

The Styx River where the grenades were found is named after the mythological stream said to flow through Hades. This small southern river at one point marks the boundary between Alabama and Florida, leading to much local humor about which side of the river is supposed to be the netherworld.

CHAPTER 3

GNUS OF THE DAY

Q: What's nu?
A: Energy divided by Planck's constant.

"How did it go?" Eric asked. "Did you catch the bad guys?"

"I don't know," Shelby said tiredly as she dropped to the sofa. "They hustled me out once the suspect named a name they all wanted to hear."

"So it was a wasted trip?"

Shelby shot an irritated glance at her husband. "No, I didn't say that. I told the police when their suspect was lying, and from that they were able to get their lead. I earned my fee."

The corners of Eric's mouth lifted slightly. "I'm sure you did, dear."

Shelby pressed her lips together and said nothing. Eric was one of those people who could make a term of endearment sound patronizing—his way of reminding her he wasn't exactly delighted with her growing reputation among the various police forces of the nation. Over and over he'd urged her to use her special gift with discretion. But whenever she'd tried to pin him down as to what he meant by "discretion," he'd ended up hinting she should keep her lie-detecting abilities secret altogether.

"Did Tee call?" she asked.

"I don't know, I just got in myself."

Shelby thought about calling her sister but couldn't summon up the energy. Why should one quick trip to Pittsburgh make her so tired? Eric was on the phone anyway, calling the neighborhood deli;

Shelby was vaguely glad he'd taken the initiative. "Kosher okay?" he asked.

"Of course," she answered.

When he'd hung up, he started out of the room but abruptly turned back. He bent over the sofa and kissed her lightly. "I can see you're tired," he said in his nice-Eric voice. "Put your feet up and take it easy. I'm going to take a shower." He switched on the television for her before he left.

A singing commercial urged Shelby to be sure to take all her income tax deductions. "Dew it for the wahhns yew luh-huv," the singers intoned. "Go awn—dew it."

The adenoidal singers gave way to a newscaster who acted beautifully his role of well-informed and deeply concerned Purveyor of Truth. He gazed sincerely into the camera lens as he explained the American government's latest inflationary counter-spiral program. Shelby drifted in and out of sleep.

And came fully awake. The newscaster was saying:

> . . . that the Honduran uprising failed because virtually all the weapons carried by the rebels were defective. The Hondurans were armed with lightweight .30 caliber carbines. These carbines are shortened infantry rifles first introduced by the U. S. Army during World War II and which have long since been superseded by more effective weapons such as the M-16 rifles. Almost all the carbines recovered from the Honduran insurrectionists had faulty spring mechanisms that prevented the rifles from firing. UN Intelligence is currently attempting to trace the source of these obsolete weapons.
>
> In Washington today . . .

Something teased at Shelby's memory as Eric came back in from his shower. Then she remembered. "Eric, that's the second time today—hm, you smell good—that there's been something in the news about defective weapons. Somebody dumped a bunch of useless grenades in some little southern river just a few days ago."

"Oh, really?" Not interested.

"But the strange thing is that both times the weapons were obsolete. Dating from the Second World War. Where have they been all this time? Why would anyone hold on to defective old weapons?"

"Who knows? Life is just full of little mysteries."

Shelby sighed. The cliché was true. Like she never would know what was in that package the Loser had passed on to Wee Willie Bascomb at the Oyster House in Pittsburgh.

"Where is that delivery boy?" Eric said irritably. "They told me half an hour."

"It hasn't been that long. The news just went off."

"They're only down the block, for Chrissake. Shouldn't take more than ten or fifteen minutes."

"What's the matter? Why're you so grouchy?"

"Missed lunch today. I couldn't get away from the office."

Shelby turned her head away from the pulsating red aura around her husband's body that told her he was lying. It was beginning to dawn on her that it wasn't the trip to Pittsburgh but coming home that had made her so tired.

CHAPTER 4

SOME OF THE PEOPLE
ALL OF THE TIME

Mouths without hands; maintained at vast expense,
In peace a charge, in war a weak defense.

—John Dryden, "Lines on a Paid
Militia" from *Cymon and Iphigenia*

Shelby Kent and many others had wondered at the simultaneous appearance in the news of two batches of defective, obsolete weapons. She, and many others, had speculated vaguely over a possible connection between the worthless rifles in Honduras and the dud grenades in the River Styx. They all thought about it awhile, and then they forgot it.

Sir John Dudley didn't forget. It was Sir John's job not to overlook or ignore or forget anything that involved the United Nations Militia. It was his office's intelligence reports that had warned the commanding officer in Tegucigalpa that trouble was brewing in San Pedro. And it was his responsibility to sniff out the next place and time terrorists would get hold of illegal weapons. For it was going to happen again, he was sure of it. All the signs said so.

The distinctions between war and peace had been growing increasingly vague over the years—battle took place under an ever-expanding variety of labels ranging from "police action" to "defensive strike." The Asian wars of the fifties and sixties had demonstrated dramatically that hand-to-hand combat still had advantages over nuclear warfare—the old chestnut about not firing off a cannon to kill a gnat. Korea, for example, had been an infantry war.

Thus the infantryman made a return to one of his traditional roles. Throughout history the foot soldier had been called upon to back up civil authority; this civil-military alliance came to be taken for granted in the second half of the twentieth century as one deadly encounter after another was fought at street level. Belfast became the world's symbol for the horrors of blood in the streets, and the warrior-policeman was more and more in demand because of his training in riot control. The UN Militiaman, wearing his lightweight plastic armor and carrying his modern weapons, was a figure to be feared and respected.

When the nations of the world had finally agreed that a full-time, sophisticated, international peacekeeping force was essential to global stability, Sir John Dudley had been plucked from retirement to head up the Militia's intelligence operation. He was the logical choice for the job. Sir John had been a very young man when the Nazi fungus had begun spreading over Europe. He'd spent the war at Bletchley, part of the British government's oddball collection of code-crackers and decipherers. Eventually the mathematicians and the linguists and the classical dons and the solvers of crossword puzzles who made up the Government Code and Cipher School had drifted back to their normal lives. But young John Dudley, intrigued by the whole spy-catching business, had stayed on in MI-6, to the Foreign Office's undisguised delight. He'd risen to become Chief of Secret Intelligence Service, accumulating along the way the expertise that had caused the UN to summon him from a predictably dull retirement. A worldwide intelligence system—with muscle to back it up. How could he resist?

Interpol had never had any real clout because of its dependence upon the voluntary co-operation of local law enforcement officers. But an intelligence operation tied to an international militia would be both co-ordinated and on safe legal ground everywhere in the world. A committee of UN delegates had labored for three years to draw up the plans for a military organization that would not be tied up in red tape when crossing international boundaries but which would still respect the rights of individual nations.

Not an easy task. And not one all the peoples of the world were in sympathy with. A global army? they asked. What a weapon for totalitarian oppression. Not at all, said others. The UN system of checks and balances was such as to make hegemony impossible—no one group of people could ever effectively gain dominance over another group of people. But things never were really that simple, so people still worried. And large numbers simply weren't sure how they felt about it at all.

For that reason Sir John Dudley and his intelligence operatives had to tread carefully. The first act of rebellion, in Burma, had been treated as a purely local matter, puzzling but not particularly significant. There had been very little news coverage of the event—reporters weren't noticeably eager to parachute into the Burmese jungles and had contented themselves with official handouts. The second incident, in Honduras, had been much more visible. And then there was that curious business of the grenades in the Styx River. (The Styx! What on earth had possessed the Americans to name it that?)

What the general public didn't know was that the insurrectionists in Burma had also been armed with defective weapons.

Sir John stared out the window of his office, seeing nothing of New York's busyness below him. Burma, Honduras, Alabama—where was the pattern? Not even a geographic balance: once in Asia, twice in the Americas. Where next—Africa, Europe? The North Pole? He snorted. A rebellion of Eskimos? Not bloody likely.

Two questions needed answering. One, what did the insurrectionists think they were going to accomplish? Two, why were acts of rebellion undertaken with weapons that virtually guaranteed failure? Sir John suspected the first question was not particularly important—sometimes any excuse for a fight would do. Survivors of the Burmese fiasco had all been members of a splinter sect of one of those esoteric Eastern religions that were a constant source of unrest. The conflict was an old one: *You go to my church and I'll go to mine—or else I'll kill you.* For some reason the insurrectionists had thought attacking a UN garrison on the Irrawaddy was a good way to force their own religious views on the rest of the country. Sir John had not yet received a final report on what the Honduran rebels thought they were fighting for.

Of much more interest was the question of the weapons. The World War II .30 caliber carbines the Hondurans had been carrying—some of them still bore traces of their original packing grease. Incredible. Where had they been all these years? And even if the carbines had not been defective, did the Hondurans really believe they would be effective against the more sophisticated weaponry used by the UN Militia? At short range the carbine was deadly, but shoot at a distant target and it became totally unreliable. The carbine fired a bullet with only a third of the energy and two-thirds the velocity of most standard service rifles. Many of the American states had banned the carbine's use in hunting because it wounded more game than it killed. The .30 caliber carbine was little more than a high-powered pistol. The only explanation for its appearance in the hands of the Honduran insurgents was that they didn't know the difference.

Two shipments of military hardware that wouldn't work might be dismissed as coincidence, but the bad grenades that had showed up in Alabama—well, that changed the picture considerably. Coincidence was out. The only difference was that the Americans had detected the flaws in their weapons whereas the Burmese and the Hondurans had not. But then, Americans always had been handy with instruments of destruction. Southern Alabama was now witnessing an influx of UN Militia and intelligence agents large enough to discourage even the most dedicated of rebels. Alabama wasn't the problem.

The problem was who was supplying these useless weapons, and why? Did there exist somewhere some benevolent masked marvel who saw himself as a defender of the world's attempt to protect itself against itself? Was there someone who'd learned in advance of the insurgents' intentions and then took steps to make sure they failed? One could indeed argue that whoever had supplied those weapons had helped the UN's peacekeeping efforts in the world. Petty rebellions sometimes had a nasty way of growing into major revolutions.

The intercom on his desk buzzed. "Mr. Gilbert to see you, Sir John."

"Send him in."

Kevin Gilbert's normally tanned face had a gray look to it, which Sir John knew meant he hadn't had much sleep. Gilbert was one of those Americans who took a workaday approach to every problem they encountered, no matter how outré. It was Gilbert Sir John had sent to Honduras to find out what was going on.

"Well?" asked Sir John. "What's the final count?"

"As of last night, six hundred thirteen Hondurans dead, two Militia."

"That's two too many."

"Most of the Hondurans were killed in the first rocket attack," Gilbert said. "The CO stopped the second launching when he saw the insurgents weren't doing much in the way of hitting back. So he just sent in mop-up squads, and that was the end of it. A lot of yelling and cursing, but the Hondurans couldn't really do anything when most of their weapons wouldn't fire."

Sir John nodded. "I want to know why over six hundred people just died."

"Political reasons this time, not religious ones. Free the people. Kill the UN slave-masters. Kill the dictator. Kill the tax assessor. Kill the postman."

"Have a pew."

Gilbert sat down and made his report. Extensive interrogation of the survivors had revealed a lot of slogans but very little in the way of hard facts. "One of them kept yelling, 'Death to the tyrants! Death to the tyrants!' When we asked him *which* tyrants, he couldn't name a single name."

"Your conclusion?"

"These rebels are the kind who'll hit out at any established power. They were planning an attack on the UN forces in Tegucigalpa when we learned of the arms shipments to San Pedro and stole a march on them. The fact that it happened to be the UN Militia they were after is almost incidental. Any bastion of authority would have done."

Sir John himself had been thinking earlier that sometimes any excuse for a fight would do. Gilbert was probably right: any target would do, as well. "What about the supplier?"

Gilbert shook his head. "Nothing. The only two of the leaders who weren't killed said they'd dealt with a man named Pedro, no last name."

"Pedro as in San Pedro?"

"Yes, sir. False name, obviously, as well as incomplete. We're trying to trace him—but it's the needle in the haystack. How many Pedros are there in Central America?"

Sir John nodded, his attention already elsewhere; he'd expected nothing else. He walked over and stood in front of the map of the world that covered the wall opposite his desk. "You think it will happen again?" he said to Gilbert.

"I'd bet on it," Gilbert answered. "And I'd give next month's salary to know why."

Sir John stared at the map. "Where?"

"Africa," Gilbert said without hesitation.

"Why Africa?"

"Because the one time faulty weapons were supplied to a non-Third-World group, it didn't work. Next time our supplier will stick to people with little experience with modern weaponry. Or near-modern. That means a nonindustrialized people. Hill people in Afghanistan. Nomadic herdsmen almost anywhere. But African tribes are more populous and more easily accessible than wandering goatherds. I say Africa."

"You may be right," Sir John said darkly.

CHAPTER 5

I'VE GOT A LITTLE LISZT

"He does it on purpose," Shelby Kent complained to her sister. "He deliberately tells me a lie, and then watches to see what I'll do."

"What do you do?" Tee asked.

"Pretend not to notice. Have to, now—only way to avoid a fight. Oh, I took the bait when he first started doing it. And we had quite a few knock-down-drag-outs, I can tell you. Eric *wants* to fight with me, Tee. So he keeps setting these little traps."

"Which you keep sidestepping. How long can you keep that up?"

"Not much longer," Shelby sighed. "Confrontation Time looms. You know he wants me to give up the police work."

"You're not going to, are you?"

"I thought about it. For a full five minutes, I thought about it. But hell, Tee, I'm the only person in the world who can read that particular aura people give off when they're lying. I should give up my one claim to uniqueness just because Eric Kent can't handle it? It's a valuable gift—I didn't ask for it, I didn't work for it. I was born with it. But I'm not going to let Eric bully me into giving it up."

"Ah, come on, Shel," Tee said unhappily. "You're both reasonable people. You'll work it out."

Shelby looked at her sister's face and felt a stab of remorse. She had no business dumping her marital problem on Tee; Tee herself had retreated into marriage as a refuge against the mean hard cold ugly competitive world that intimidated her utterly.

"What's on this afternoon?" Shelby asked, changing the subject.

Tee made a face. "*Giselle*. Tinkle, tinkle, plonk, plonk. Sometimes I think I'll go mad if I have to play that insipid stuff one more time."

Every day at noon Tee got into a cab and rode forty-one blocks downtown to the dingy loft the Metropolitan Ballet Company used as a rehearsal hall. There she sat at an upright piano for four hours, pounding out tunes that bored her stiff while the dancers bent and stretched and leaped and sometimes fell down. Then into another cab (Tee claimed that every bus she'd ever boarded had had at least six crazy people on it) and back home again to wait for her husband. Mornings were good; Tee could play her real music, practice scales, teach herself, improve and grow—a concert pianist who didn't give concerts. Tee was afraid. Of almost everything. Her piano, her husband, and her sister were the three points of the triangle that enclosed her life.

Hiding her light under a bushel, Shelby thought. *Exactly what Eric wants me to do.*

"What about you?" Tee asked. "Any more police jobs lined up?"

"I never know until the last minute. I just get a call and somebody says they've got a suspect and could I come listen. That's why I have so few jobs on the west coast—they can hold a suspect only so long without charging him, and sometimes I just can't get there fast enough."

"Oh sure—I never thought of that. They wouldn't know ahead of time who's going to be a suspect, would they? I didn't realize you have to be ready to pick up and go at any time."

"It's not too bad. I keep a bag packed, just in case I have to stay overnight."

All the time they were talking Tee kept squeezing a pair of hand grips, contraptions made of tough plastic handles and stiff metal coils. Tee had begun hand-strengthening exercises almost from the day she'd discovered what a piano was—with the result that the unathletic Tee now had the strongest hands of anyone Shelby knew. Whenever there was a jar with a tight lid that needed opening, it was Tee who did the opening.

"My agent got a call yesterday," Tee said offhandedly, squeezing away.

"Oh?" Shelby perked up.

"New Orleans Symphony. Wanted to know if I was still available."

"Tee . . ."

"I said maybe next year."

"Oh, Tee!"

"Can't do it, Shelby. I'm just not ready."

"The hell you aren't! You—"

"I can't. I just can't. But it's nice to know you're remembered. Maybe next year."

"Tee." Shelby used her stern-older-sister voice. "You've been saying that for over two years now. It's time you came out of hiding. Professionally, you're ready. You've got to stop making excuses. *You've got to stop being scared.*"

"Next year," said Tee. "I promise."

Shelby's phone rang. "Yes . . . yes, Sergeant. Twenty-fifth Precinct. Yes, I remember where the station is—on 119th, right? Be there in half an hour." She replaced the receiver. "Got to run. They've picked up some guy in East Harlem guarding an arsenal big enough to equip a small army."

CHAPTER 6

HOLD THAT LINE

Two Men of Steel Comment on Their Profession

Everything that happens in the game happens for the best. Regardless of all the things that are said and written during the season, I'm almost always able to walk tall. I've got the most powerful force a man can have on his side—God.

—Mel Blount

Pro football is the enema of society. There's an element of society that uses football as a release. There's one Steelers fan who sits behind the bench at home games and berates Dwight White for four quarters. I figure it must be some kind of therapy for that fan to scream at White.

—Randy Grossman

Eric Kent stared at the list he had just made out and swept it aside in disgust. Free Jersey Day. Free Helmet Day. Free Kick-in-the-Ass Day.

You couldn't *bribe* people into supporting a losing team. That's what baseball tried to do—but baseball had a 162-game schedule and interest was bound to flag now and then. Football was different.

The Jets had gone seven and nine this last season. The worse they played, the more the fans stayed away. The more the fans stayed away, the more the owners screamed at Eric to *do something*. What could he do? Nobody went to a football game with an objective eye, interested only in game-playing strategy. They went to take sides, to align themselves with one team against another. To fight in a surrogate war without getting hurt. So who wanted to side with losers? How could Eric pump up any enthusiasm for a team that completed only one pass out of every four, fumbled every third time they ran the ball, and missed twenty-five-yard field goals?

Laughter in the hallway interrupted his train of thought. Eric got up and opened his door, welcoming the distraction. Three men were walking toward him, a stranger flanked by two members of the Jets organization.

"Hey, Kent, we were coming to see you," said Warren Hubbs, one of the assistant assistant coaches. "This is Bill Malone, new sports writer at the *Daily News*." Eric eyed Malone carefully as they shook hands. Parrot or adversary? Most of them were one or the other, though they all thought they were somewhere in between.

"Hubbs tells me you're the man to answer my questions," Malone said.

"Do my best." Eric smiled. "Have a seat."

Hubbs and the other Jets man, Buck Walters, took the two comfortable seats in Eric's office and left the aluminum-and-orange-plastic chair for Malone. The writer started asking beginner-type questions that Eric fielded easily, with Buck and Hubbs contributing anecdotes now and then. The atmosphere was congenial, and the three pros soon succeeded in putting the newcomer at ease. Malone was eager to make contacts within the Jets organization, and eager not to appear eager. A pussycat.

"I thought during the off-season would be a good time for me to get acquainted with the players," Malone was saying. "I've been working in San Francisco for the last six years, so I don't know many of the Jets personally. What I'd like to do is go to their homes, the ones who live in New York—interview them with their wives, that sort of thing."

Buck Walters muttered something under his breath and Warren Hubbs snickered. Eric hoped Malone wouldn't notice.

He didn't. "Could that be arranged? And maybe phone interviews with the ones who don't live in New York?"

"No problem," Eric said. "Let me check on where everybody is, and I'll get a list to you. Two, three days. That all right?"

"That's fine," said Malone, beaming. "And thanks."

"The players' wives are gonna be kinda tame next to Kent's wife," Hubbs said, and Buck guffawed.

Malone looked surprised. "Why's that?"

"Kent's wife is a mind-reader." Hubbs grinned. "She knows everything he's thinking."

"Shelby can't read minds," Eric said mildly. "That's nonsense."

"She knows when you're lying. That's the same thing as reading minds."

Malone smiled easily, still not understanding. "Like my grandmother. I never could fool her."

"Naw, that's not it," Buck said. "Kent's wife really can tell when people are lying. They give off some kind of halo or something that she can see. Nobody else can see it, but *she* can. Don't ever try to slip one over on Kent's wife. She'll call you a liar to your face."

Malone's eyes grew big, his mouth dropped open.

"Shelby's not as tactless as you are, Buck," Eric laughed, trying to keep it light. "She knows everybody lies. Hell, we all know that."

"She sees a halo around people?" Malone didn't know whether to believe Buck or not.

"An aura. A sort of red glow people give off when they're not telling the truth. It's a very special gift."

Hubbs sniggered. "The cops think so. They're always getting her to come in and tell 'em who's lying and who ain't. Tell him about the cops."

Buck laughed *haw haw haw*. "You must lead one hell of a life, Kent. Never able to lie to your wife! I'd shoot myself."

Stop this, stop it right now. "You probably want to interview the coaches too," Eric said briskly to Malone. "I'll see that their addresses are on the list as well."

"Appreciate it," Malone said, his eyes gleaming. "But I think I'd like to start off with a story about *you*."

Buck and Hubbs roared at that.

CHAPTER 7

POR FAVOR

*Follow the enemy and try to prevent
the enemy carrying away the guns.*

—Lord Raglan, much to his regret,
25 October 1854

"Do you understand Spanish?" Sergeant Delgado asked Shelby.

"Not a word. But it won't matter—the aura will show just the same. But we'll have to work out some sort of signal system so I can let you know when he's lying."

The Sergeant thought a moment. "All right, I'm going to take you into the interrogation room with me. Sit at the table with your hands in your lap. When he's lying, put one arm on the table. Got it? Let's go."

The next half hour was one of the dullest Shelby ever sat through. She followed Sergeant Delgado into the interrogation room and sat down at a long table, at the end away from the Puerto Rican prisoner to whom she was not introduced. All she knew about him was that his name was Martinez and he'd been acting as an armed watchman at a warehouse filled with weapons. For thirty minutes Shelby listened to a rapid-fire exchange of sounds that meant nothing to her. Her hands stayed in her lap.

Sergeant Delgado called a recess. Outside the interrogation room he said, "Not a single lie? Nobody can talk for half an hour without telling *some* lies."

"This guy can."

"Maybe your, uh, vision isn't working today?"

"It isn't a vision. And it's working." Shelby smiled, watching a red-glowing policeman talking on the phone.

Delgado followed her glance and grinned. "Okay, maybe I'm not asking the right questions. Let's try again."

"First tell me what he's been saying."

"He says he was just doing a favor for a friend—a favor he was getting paid for. The friend's name is Pedro, last name unknown, address unknown. But Martinez says he's a good friend." The Sergeant grunted. "Some friend."

"What are you going to do?"

"Accept his story, since you're sure he's not lying. I'll ask him where he first met Pedro, how often he sees him, that kind of stuff. What I really want to know is whether those weapons were meant to be used here in New York or if that warehouse is just a transit stop."

"For shipment overseas?"

"It's possible. But Martinez says he doesn't know what the stuff was to be used for, or where."

The second half hour wasn't much more productive than the first. Martinez began sneaking glances at Shelby, at last beginning to wonder why she was there. Shelby caught him in one lie, about his immigration visa. But all of Sergeant Delgado's other questions got completely truthful answers. The man simply saw no reason to lie.

The door to the interrogation room opened and a woman stepped in. "Luis," she said, gesturing with her head. Sergeant Delgado followed her out with Shelby trailing close behind, not wanting to stay alone with Martinez.

The woman was introduced as Sergeant Gravitz. "Report's in on the contents of the warehouse," she said. "A real mishmash. One crate of M-16 automatic rifles, fully functional. Thirty crates of Soviet AK-47 assault rifles. Seventy-five crates of the British GPMG." The policewoman flipped a page of the report. "That stands for General Purpose Machine Gun."

"What else?" asked Delgado.

"Sixty-two crates of West German MG 42-59s," Sergeant Gravitz went on. "Eighty-six crates of Israeli Uzis—"

"What?" Shelby interrupted.

"Uzi. *U, z, i.* A submachine gun with a folding metal stock, says here. Also, four crates of assorted handguns, mostly American."

Delgado: "Ammo?"

"Lots. But it wouldn't do anybody any good. Get this—except for the one crate of M-16s, none of this stuff will fire. Bunch of junk. No revolution with *these* weapons."

Sergeant Delgado whistled. "So the M-16s were used to make the sale and the rest is a rip-off."

"It's not even that clean," said Sergeant Gravitz. "These M-16s are early models, the kind used before the kinks were ironed out. The report says the first M-16s jammed a lot, and one of the things they did to help correct that was to chrome plate the chamber. These M-16s don't have any chrome plating. So while they're *functional*— that is, they could probably be fired okay in a demonstration—they wouldn't be too dependable in an actual battle. That means there's not one really good weapon in the entire warehouse."

"Again!" Shelby gasped.

Sergeant Gravitz shot her a questioning look but Delgado was nodding. "Just like Honduras," he said. "And that little town in Alabama. I wish I knew what the hell was going on."

"What happens now?" the policewoman asked.

"Now," said Sergeant Delgado, "I go back in there and convince Señor Martinez that he's going to be dragged before a UN tribunal and charged with high treason unless he helps us find his good friend Pedro."

CHAPTER 8

THE MULBERRY BUSH AS
CENTER OF THE UNIVERSE

The cream-colored program read:

The St. Louis Jaycees present
MARTITA FLEMING
in recital

Tee sighed and slipped the program back into the desk drawer. St. Louis: the last time she'd ever played before a paying audience, a little over two years ago. Two years. It was easy for Shelby to say *Stop being scared*. She didn't know what performing in public was like. It was Naked Time, and there was no way of making Shelby or anyone else who'd never experienced it understand what it was like.

Tee wasn't even Martita Fleming any more. She was Martita Bradley. The first time she'd ever seen Max Bradley had been on television, on the Tony Awards show. Max had accepted the award for best scene design and had showed more poise than the professional performers who'd followed him. Tee had been impressed.

Four A.M. Tee hated technical rehearsals; they often kept Max at the theater all night. Lights had to be set and adjusted, music cues tested, scenery changes and projections rehearsed over and over and over until they moved smooth as clockwork. The week before a play opened was always the worst.

The week after opening was only a little bit better. Max said he'd never worked on a play yet that had been ready by opening night. But by the second or third week, Max's obligations to the production would have been fulfilled and Tee would have her husband all to herself for a while. Then it would start all over again.

At last the sound of a key scraping in a lock. Tee quickly unfastened the other five locks from the inside and pulled the door open.

Max's tired face looked pleased. "Hey, hon, you didn't have to wait up."

Tee laughed. "You always say that. I wanted to. What do *you* want? Food, booze, bath . . . ?"

"You," he said, reaching for her.

When the alarm went off at ten the next morning Max was still dead to the world. Tee hated to wake him, but he was due at the theater by eleven. Tee pulled on jeans and a sweater that had shrunk when she washed it and steered her puffy-eyed husband toward the shower.

She was just pouring the coffee when Max stumbled in, told her he liked her new sweater, and lowered himself gingerly into a chair. He reached for the coffee and glowered at the boiled egg he'd asked for but didn't really want.

When he was on his second cup of the bitter coffee, Tee brought up the thing that had been bothering her. "Max, Shelby and Eric are having trouble."

Max didn't look particularly surprised. "It's the lie-detecting business, isn't it? I thought I saw that coming."

"Eric wants her to give up her police work."

"She's not going to, is she?"

"No."

"Good." Max put down his cup. "She shouldn't have to give it up. But I can see Eric's side of it. It must get to him, sometimes. He can't even tell *kind* lies—'Nice dress,' that sort of thing. Has to be a strain on him."

"But that's not it—he never complained about that. It's only when Shelby started working with the police that the trouble began. Shelby's gift—well, it's as if everything was all right so long as other people didn't know about it. As if it were something to be ashamed of."

"Oh, now—"

"Really, Max. Eric can't stand people talking about it. And if Shelby has to choose between police work and Eric, she's going to choose the police work."

"Is she that dedicated to law enforcement?"

"She's that dedicated to being what she is. She can't retreat from the whole thing and pretend she's just like everybody else."

"An admirable philosophy," Max said pointedly, "and one I wish *both* the Fleming sisters would follow."

Tee stage-sighed and rolled her eyes.

"Call your agent," Max urged, more concerned with Tee's problem than with Shelby's. "See if the New Orleans offer is still open."

"They want me to play Tchaikovsky," Tee said with distaste.

Max laughed. "Easier than starting off with Mozart or Bach. But I imagine even symphony orchestras are open to negotiation. Call your agent, Tee. It's time you got started again."

"You sound like Shelby."

"Don't put it off any longer—take the plunge. Call him. Today."

"Well . . ."

"Tee, you *owe* it to me to start performing in public again."

"I owe it to you?" Tee stared at him, wide-eyed. "Why?"

"Give me time, I'll think of a reason," Max said.

CHAPTER 9

WHICH BOBBY WATSON
DO YOU MEAN?

MRS. SMITH: Poor Bobby.
MR. SMITH: Which poor Bobby do you mean?
MRS. SMITH: It is his wife that I mean. She is called Bobby too, Bobby Watson. Since they both had the same name, you could never tell one from the other when you saw them together. It was only after his death that you could really tell which was which. And there are still people today who confuse her with the deceased and offer their condolences to him.

—Eugène Ionesco, *The Bald Soprano*

"So I was wrong about Africa," said Kevin Gilbert.

"Not necessarily," Sir John Dudley replied. "If those weapons were meant for New York, why were they kept sitting in a warehouse for two weeks until the police arrested Martinez? They would have been moved long before that. I'd say there was a hitch in the transportation arrangements somewhere along the line. This Pedro, whoever he is, could well have been trying to find cargo space aboard an eastbound freighter when the New York police found Martinez instead."

"What about our check of the waterfront?"

"We have a couple of possible leads—difficult to be certain, when all we have to go on is that our man is Latin and may or may not be calling himself Pedro. It may come to nothing. Pedro won't be showing his face at the waterfront or anywhere else for a while."

"Who the hell is this guy anyway?" Gilbert said with irritation. "How could he get away with arming terrorists in remote spots in Burma and Honduras and then blow it in East Harlem? He's been damned efficient up to now."

"Perhaps it's not the same chap. Isn't it possible that 'Pedro' is just a code name for, well, 'middleman'? Or more likely, one of several code names. 'Pedro' would be right at home with Hondurans and expatriate Puerto Ricans. But in Burma? Or southern Alabama? Doesn't seem likely, does it?"

"A code name for 'middleman'?" Gilbert repeated slowly. "That would imply a very large organization at work."

"So it would," Sir John agreed. "Can you really believe that one man is doing all this? Even with a large staff working for him? How could one man know about potential trouble spots in the world, locate the obsolete weapons, make a deal with the terrorists, arrange the shipments, and then walk away as anonymously as he came? Only on your American telly do such rich and powerful villains exist, commanding armies of human robots that carry out every command without question. In reality things are more likely to be decided in committee. Our picture of the anarchist building bombs in his basement is a thing of the past."

"You're saying conspiracy."

"I'm saying conspiracy. Can we be sure that the Pedro who showed up in Harlem is the same Pedro we're hunting in Honduras? How many Pedros are there? Here, take a look at this," Sir John said abruptly, handing Gilbert a manila file folder.

It was a trace report on the defective weaponry. The arms supplied to the Burmese terrorists had been part of a shipment believed to have been captured by the Japanese during World War II. The defective firing pins in the Alabama grenades had been detected by U.S. military personnel in 1943; the grenades were on record as having been destroyed. U. S. Army records also listed the carbines that had surfaced in Honduras as "lost in transit." The history of the weapons stored in the New York warehouse had not yet been determined.

"Lost in transit!" said Gilbert, appalled. "The Army *loses* a shipment of rifles and doesn't follow up on it?"

" 'Lost in transit' is a military euphemism," Sir John said. "The rifles were stolen. The Army knew they were worthless and were shipping them back to the manufacturer when hijackers made off with them. Someone in authority simply figured good riddance and closed the file."

Gilbert grunted.

"The Harlem weapons all date from the time of the Asian wars, and they'll undoubtedly turn out to be mislaid or captured as well," Sir John went on. "See the beauty of it? No single supplier, no way to trace the buyer. Just little piles of leftover weaponry here and there in the world. Some Oriental village must have been delighted to make a little money on the useless hardware left behind by the retreating Japanese soldiers. The report says the Burma weapons show signs of saline corrosion—which means they'd been sitting somewhere near the sea all these years since the war ended. On one of those little South Pacific islands, perhaps. Or a harbor town on the China Sea."

Gilbert was frowning. "So somebody—or several somebodies, if your conspiracy theory is right—right now somebody is searching the world for defective weaponry."

"Which brings us to the next point. Just how many mislaid old weapons can there be? The source has to be a limited one—our conspirators don't have an unending supply of rusty rifles to draw upon. What do they do then?"

"Buy new ones."

"Exactly. What do munitions manufacturers do with their clinkers? Even with modern manufacturing methods there must be an occasional batch of duds. What arms manufacturer would turn down the chance to recover part of his investment?"

"So the conspirators would start contacting munitions manufacturers as their supply of old weapons ran out." Gilbert mused a moment. "Even if no contact has been made yet, we can warn the manufacturers to be on the lookout for inquiries about their rejects."

"Quite. See that it's laid on, will you, Gilbert?"

Gilbert translated "laid on" into "arranged" and said, "Right away, sir."

Sir John's phone rang. He said "Yes?", listened ten seconds, said "Thank you," and hung up the phone.

"That was the New York police," he told Gilbert. "They have Pedro."

CHAPTER 10

A FAR, FAR BETTER THING

"This Pedro," Shelby was saying to Eric, "may have been the same man who supplied the Honduran rebels with *their* defective arms. If that's the case, UN Intelligence will take over the investigation."

"Then you'll be out of it?"

"Almost certainly."

Eric didn't say *Thank God for that;* it wasn't necessary. Shelby knew what he was thinking.

"Was Tee here today?" Eric asked.

"Yes. Why?"

"She left one of her accouterments behind." He held up one of Tee's hand grips. "Will she be needing it tonight?"

"No, she has half a dozen of those things. I'll drop it off when I get back."

Eric was trying out the hand grip. First he tried one hand, then the other. Then he tried both together, until he was grimacing from the effort. "My God, how does she do it? I can't make this thing close even with both hands!"

Shelby laughed. "You'd have to be the strong man in the circus to do that. Tee gets those grips made to order. None of the regular commercial hand grips have coils tight enough to do her any good."

Eric put down the grip and shook his hands to get rid of the sting. "What time are you leaving tomorrow?"

"About eight. Dr. Wedner said count on two days, so I'll be back around dinnertime Thursday."

"Are you staying with the Wedners?"

"Yes, as usual."

"New Brunswick isn't that far. Why not just drive back tomorrow night?"

"The two days include one night session. Either that, or stretch it out to three days."

Eric nodded, familiar with Dr. Wedner's working habits. Wedner was one of those scientists who just kept going until somebody could make them understand it was time to stop for a while. "What kind of new instrument is it he wants to test?"

"It's supposed to measure my neurological responses to different shades of the same color. Red in my case, of course."

"I thought they ran that test last year."

"They tried to, but the testing instrument wasn't up to it. This is a new improved model."

Eric grunted. "Sounds like something advertised on television. Well, I hope it isn't too tedious for you."

"I'm used to it by now." Shelby had been making the short drive down to the Rutgers campus off and on for almost four years so Dr. Wedner and his staff could learn everything they could about her aura-reading ability. She'd read a dozen articles about herself in scientific journals in which she was referred to only as "the subject" —the good doctor's attempt to shield her against undesirable public-ity. But Shelby herself had sabotaged that strategy when she began working with the New York police. Then at police conventions and such the NYPD had passed on the word that one Shelby Kent was more accurate than voice stress analysis and polygraph combined— and the rush was on.

Eric wanted to talk to Shelby about something, but he decided to put it off until she got back from New Brunswick. It wouldn't be fair to dump it on her right before she left. Besides, he hadn't quite made up his mind as to the best approach to take with her.

He'd had a nibble about a new job. A man he'd lunched with had oh-so-casually let it be known that the San Diego Chargers would soon be looking for a new Director of Promotion. The man himself was an intermediary, sent to sound Eric out, to learn if he'd be inter-ested in talking about a move. Eric had tried to remain casual as he admitted the possibility might hold some interest for him.

Hold some interest for him! He'd jump at it. Here was the one thing he and Shelby needed the most—a chance to make a fresh start. A chance to get away from the sniggering and the elbowing and the jokes behind his back. A chance to get Shelby away from those sordid criminal types she was spending more and more time with. A chance to live a normal life again.

But Shelby wouldn't give it all up just because he asked her to—he knew better than that. It would be hard enough for her to leave her sister and Dr. Wedner's testing program at Rutgers. But airplanes flew west-to-east too: she could make frequent trips back. Those things could be handled. What might cause trouble was Shelby's plain old-fashioned stubbornness.

If there were only some way to make her understand what her so-called career was doing to him. *Could* a woman understand such things as the sort of shifting allegiances going on in Eric's world? He hadn't told her about that humiliating episode with Buck and Hubbs and the new sports writer. Maybe he should tell her—that might make her see. How he and Buck and Hubbs had been a team handling an outsider who could be of use to them. How her name had come into the conversation—and all of a sudden it was Buck and Hubbs and the writer versus Eric. Suddenly *he* was the outsider. And he didn't like it out there. He was a team player, had always been a team player.

Another thing. Shelby didn't like the west coast very much—in fact, she hated it. This wasn't going to be easy.

But maybe nothing would come of it anyway. Friday Eric had an appointment with a man fairly high up in the Chargers hierarchy; he'd know where he stood a little better after that. If the prospects looked good, he'd tell Shelby about it this weekend. This weekend, yes, that was better.

In the meantime, he still had the Jets to worry about. Eric needed something to hype season-ticket sales. The competition for the entertainment dollar got a little fiercer every year, and people in Eric's profession were reduced to thinking up gimmick after gimmick after gimmick.

Maybe a new mascot?

CHAPTER 11

OUT ON A LIMBO

There was a young man from Japan,
Whose limericks never would scan.
When told this was so,
He replied, "Yes, I know,
But I always try to get as many words into the last line as ever
I possibly can."

New York *Times:*

Arrest Made in East
Harlem Arsenal Case

Police yesterday arrested Pedro Yglesias, no address, in connection with the storage of weapons and ammunition in a 114th Street warehouse. Juan Martinez, apprehended by police last week, claims Yglesias hired him to guard the warehouse and provided him with sidearms for that purpose.

Yglesias denies all knowledge of the warehouse and its contents. Almost all of the stored weapons are defective, according to Police Sgt. Luis Delgado.

. . . but Senator Bromfield says the accusation of improper conduct is politically motivated.

On the local scene, Pedro Yglesias, the man police say amassed an arsenal of useless weapons in East Harlem, is in a little deeper tonight. Captain J. S. Gulbransen of the freighter Margarita *bound for Capetown, South Africa,*

says Yglesias tried to bribe him into taking on cargo ille-
gally. Captain Gulbransen has identified Yglesias as the
man who approached him about shipping a number of
crates without the freight forwarding documentation re-
quired by federal and international law. Gulbransen said
Yglesias claimed the crates contained Japanese motorcycle
parts. Yglesias is still denying any knowledge of the arse-
nal. Last year Captain Gulbransen was charged with smug-
gling by the Treasury Department, but those charges were
later dropped.

Elsewhere in the news . . .

Eric: "Any chance they'll call you in to listen to whatsisname, Yglesias?"
Shelby: "They don't need me. They already know he's lying."

TWX 24.6/9B UNIA HQ ATTN SIR JOHN DUDLEY BOTH SURVIVING HONDURAN LEADERS POST PHOTO IDENT PEDRO YGLESIAS SUPPLIER DEFEC ARMS RPT FOLLOWS

Sir John: "Only one Pedro after all. And he didn't even bother to use a false name. He was either very sure of himself or very amateurish. Amounts to the same thing in the long run. You were right about Africa, Gilbert—that was the next stop. Now we need to know who gave Pedro Yglesias his orders. He's held out longer than I thought he would."
Gilbert: "Lean on him a little?"
Sir John: "A little."

UN Ambassador Implicated
In Defective Arms Plot

NEW YORK (AP)—Pedro Yglesias, alleged entrepreneur of defective weaponry, has told UN Intelligence officers he was acting under the direct orders of Mañuel Aguirrez, head of the Mexican delegation to the United Nations, when he supplied terrorists with arms and ammunition.

According to Yglesias, Ambassador Aguirrez has ordered the

illegal shipment of arms three times. Yglesias, a Mexican national, claims he arranged transportation in each case without knowing the weapons' point of origin.

The first shipment was of rifles and ammunition from New York to Honduras. The weapons had been stolen from a U. S. Army supply train in 1943. Yglesias claims Ambassador Aguirrez arranged the purchase of the rifles while Yglesias was responsible for their delivery.

Yglesias also admits shipping defective grenades to Seminole, Alabama, again disclaiming knowledge of their source. Yglesias was trying to arrange shipment of weapons to Capetown, South Africa, when he was arrested.

After admitting complicity in three illegal shipments, Yglesias denied supplying arms to Burmese insurgents last February. UN Intelligence confirms that the Burmese weapons were also defective.

Ambassador Aguirrez could not be reached for comment.

CHAPTER 12

EVERY MAN IN HIS HUMIDOR

Our researchers into Public Opinion are content
That he held the proper opinions for the time of year;
When there was peace, he was for peace; when there was
*   war, he went.*

—W. H. Auden, "The Unknown Citizen"

"He lost his papers," Kevin Gilbert said. "That's what happened."

"His papers?" Sir John frowned.

"His shipping papers. Yglesias says Ambassador Aguirrez provided him with shipping papers—probably forged—and he lost the ones for the Harlem weapons. The ones intended for Africa."

Sir John shook his head in amazement. "So then he goes out and makes that clumsy attempt at bribing the captain?"

"Yes, sir," said Gilbert, not stating the obvious.

Sir John stated it. "Hardly jibes with my idea of a super-efficient organization at work, does it? I still smell conspiracy, but this Pedro Yglesias . . . the man's a fool. What did he do—just ask around for the name of a ship's captain with a shady past?"

"That's about it. He said he was afraid to tell Aguirrez he'd lost the papers and ask for new ones. Seems he'd messed up an earlier shipment. To Peru. That one never got off the ground, fortunately for us. So rather than tell Aguirrez he'd goofed again, Yglesias tried to arrange a shipment without the papers. He's obviously an amateur —didn't know the first thing about what he was doing."

"Did he know why he was doing it? What reason did Aguirrez

give him for all this extraordinary shipping of weapons hither and yon?"

"Well, sir, he's not too clear on that. Something to do with fighting tyranny. Aguirrez told him it was all part of a top secret operation and he shouldn't ask too many questions. At least that's what Yglesias *says* Aguirrez told him."

Sir John looked disgusted. " 'Fighting tyranny'—a suitably vague phrase. You don't suppose the esteemed Mexican ambassador to the UN is in it for the money, do you? Selling worthless weapons for whatever he can get? He's going on television tonight, you know—going to deny the whole thing."

"Will it do him any good?"

"Probably not. There's talk of a Security Council commission to inquire into the matter. If it goes that far, we're going to have to come up with some hard evidence of Aguirrez's involvement."

"There are several lines of investigation we can—"

"Good, put it all in your report. I'm taking you off the arms investigation temporarily. There's somebody I want you to check out personally."

Gilbert nodded, thinking *Ambassador Aguirrez.*

"A woman named Shelby Kent," Sir John said. "Lives here in New York. Assign someone to run a security check on her. What I want you to investigate is the reliability of a rather unusual talent she has. It seems the lady is a human lie detector. The information I have is that nobody can tell her a lie and get away with it." Sir John noticed the incredulous look on Gilbert's face and smiled. "She's been working as a police consultant for a couple of years. The New York police officer who caught Pedro Yglesias swears by her."

Gilbert started to laugh but then cut the laugh off short. "A human lie detector. You mean she's a psychic?"

"Not exactly. True, some police departments still do call in psychics—to help locate missing persons or describe murderers by handling their victims' belongings or some such jiggery-pokery. This Shelby Kent doesn't do anything like that. She, ah, reads an aura that people supposedly give off when they lie. Start with Dr. Bernard Wedner at Rutgers University—he's been running tests on her. Then check the police she's worked with."

Gilbert still looked skeptical. "She reads an aura and knows when people are lying?"

"That's the word."

"Excuse me, Sir John, but that's hard to believe. Why have I never heard of her? Why hasn't she been in the news, why haven't books been written about her? That's really incredible—a human lie detector!"

"Yes, it is a bit hard to believe," Sir John admitted. "That's why I want you to investigate personally. If her talent is indeed foolproof—and I've been assured that it is—we're going to need the lady's services. As to why you've never heard of her, she simply prefers it that way. If she'd wanted to capitalize on her talent for personal fame and fortune, she certainly had the means to do so—she's married to a PR man. But only Dr. Wedner and his team and the police have known about her officially. But policemen talk, just like everybody else. Her 'secret' isn't really a secret any more."

"And you're thinking of using her . . . to question Aguirrez?"

"Possibly. I'm also thinking the Security Council's commission of inquiry might like to know about her. If it comes to that."

For the first time the thought came to Kevin Gilbert that the old man was getting senile. To get taken in by something so patently phony as a *human lie detector*—what kind of con job was this Kent woman working? What was she after? She had to be good . . . how else could she have fooled the police? So no séances or obvious show biz tricks like that. He'd find out what she did and how she did it. By God yes, he'd find out.

"Do you object to the assignment?" Sir John asked wryly.

"No sir, I welcome it," Gilbert answered grimly.

CHAPTER 13

MACHO DO ABOUT NOTHING

Eric Kent looked around the bar with distaste. Theater people. Half of them neurotic and the rest flaming homosexuals. All using their profession as an excuse for any self-indulgent gesture that appealed to them.

"Hello, sweetheart," said the carefully made-up creature standing beside him at the bar. "I haven't seen you in here before." The carefully made-up creature was male.

"Looking for someone," Eric said rudely and turned his back.

"Now, now, mustn't be uppity. Maybe I can help. Whom seek ye?"

Eric looked back at the rouged and mascaraed face and thought *what the hell*. "Max Bradley. Know him?"

"Oh, you're a friend of Max's. He'll be along in a bit. My name's Vincent. What's yours?"

"Eric Kent," said Eric, being careful to separate the hard *c* in Eric from the *K* in Kent. "Are you sure he'll be coming here?"

"Sweetheart, I just *left* him at the theater and I can *assure* you he needs a drink. He'll be here. You're not in the profession, are you? No, I thought not. How do you know Max?"

"His wife and mine are sisters." *Why am I explaining myself to this freak?*

"Oh, *family*," Vincent twinkled. "How nice. You here for a little male bonding?"

"None of your damned business what I'm here for," said Eric, exasperated.

Vincent giggled. "My, you really are a breath of stale air, aren't you? You really should learn to relax, sweetheart."

"Don't call me sweetheart." Eric was relieved to see Max come into the bar; he raised an arm and waved.

Max was surprised to see him, and even more surprised to find him with Vincent. "Hello Eric?" Making it a question.

"I thought I could catch you here. Can we talk? Privately?"

Vincent pretended to be hurt. "I was just keeping your brother-in-marriage amused until you got here," he told Max. "Now I am to be discarded like a used Kleenex. Egad." He drifted away.

"How can you work with people like that?" Eric didn't even try to hide his revulsion.

Max found Eric's reaction to Vincent depressing. "Vincent is one of the best choreographers I know," he said mildly. "The dancers love to work with him. He never gets mad, he never shouts. And he gets results."

Eric heard the note of reprimand in Max's voice and dropped the subject. "Can we get a booth?"

Max asked the bartender for a martini and led Eric to an empty booth. "Now. What's on your mind?"

Eric plunged right in. "I'm going to be offered a job with the Chargers. I had a long meeting today with some people from San Diego, and it looks good. It'll be a step up for me, and I want to take it."

"That's great, Eric," Max said, sincerely pleased for him. "Congratulations."

"But there's a problem. Shelby."

Max frowned. "I know Shelby doesn't like California, but once she gets started with the police out there—"

"*That's* the problem. She mustn't 'get started' with the police out there. It's a chance for her to break away from all that nonsense and live a normal life."

Doubledoubletoilandtrouble. "I doubt that Shelby will ever live a 'normal' life," Max said slowly. "She's unique, you know—nobody else is like her. It'd be a mistake to try to force her into a normal mode of living."

"Thanks for the advice," Eric snapped. "But I have to be the judge of what's best. Shelby's not known on the west coast. We'd have a chance out there. Max, you've got to take my word for it—it would be best if Shelby dropped her police work altogether."

Best for which one of you? Max wondered, but said nothing.

"I need your help," Eric went on. "I want you to ask Tee to talk to Shelby. Persuade her to try it my way."

"Wait a minute. You want me to ask Tee to ask Shelby to give up her police work? Why not just ask her yourself?" *Either "her."* "Why this roundabout approach?"

"Tee will listen to you, and Shelby will listen to Tee. Shelby doesn't always hear *me*," Eric said bitterly. "Look, Max, I'm trying to save my marriage. It's Shelby's aura reading that's driving us apart."

"You knew about it when you married her."

"I didn't know it would make me a laughingstock with the men I work with."

Uh-huh, that was it. "I can see how it'd be rough," Max conceded. "But surely Shelby's more important to you than they are? Couldn't you just, well, be proud of her?"

Eric's eyes were slits. "Try putting yourself in my place. How would the men you work with treat *you* if they knew you could never lie to your wife? Or are they all like Vincent?"

Max laughed, refusing to take offense. "Vincent would be fascinated. But I know what you mean. I'd be in for some ribbing."

"It's more than just ribbing. There's nothing good-natured about it." Eric paused to collect his thoughts. "You're married to a gifted woman too, but there's nothing special about her gift. No, that didn't come out right. What I mean is that as talented as Tee is, her talent is one that's shared by other people. There's no oddity connected with it. Even if she does go back to the concert stage and become the most famous pianist in the world—well, you'd be the husband of a celebrity, that's all. You wouldn't be laughed at because of it."

So Eric looked upon his wife as something of a freak. Max tried to turn the conversation. "That may happen yet. I thought I had Tee talked into accepting an engagement with the New Orleans Symphony, but she balked at the last minute. But I think she's coming round—"

"Will you ask her? To talk to Shelby?"

Max shook his head. "I can't do that, Eric. That's asking her to conspire against her own sister. You know how close they are."

"Then just tell her that I asked for her help. Let her make up her own mind."

Max thought it over. "All right, I guess I can do that. I'll tell Tee what *you* want her to do."

"That's all I ask," said Eric.

Once that was settled, the two men found they didn't have anything more to talk about. They left the bar separately, each slightly disappointed in the other.

CHAPTER 14

ECCE FEMINA

"We'd put her on retainer if we could get funding," Sergeant Luis Delgado was explaining. "As it is, we just call her in as often as the budget lets us. On a consultant basis, you understand? It's not good—too hit-and-miss. One of these days we're gonna need her real bad and she'll be out in the boonies working with some other police department."

"How come she's never mentioned in the papers?" Kevin Gilbert wanted to know.

"Her choice. It's part of our agreement that we never release her name to the news media."

"Can you put a percentage figure on her accuracy?"

"Easy," grinned Delgado. "One hundred."

"A hundred per cent accurate?"

"That's right. The way she explained it to me, it's all pretty automatic. Either that red glow is there or it isn't. She doesn't have to evaluate anything, make judgments. Just yes or no."

"But how do you know she's right all the time?" Gilbert persisted. "If she says somebody is lying, and he says he isn't—isn't that just a matter of deciding which one to believe?"

A flicker of irritation crossed the Sergeant's face. "We don't take anybody's word for anything. Shelby Kent's say-so isn't evidence. But when she tells us a suspect is lying, then we know where to *look* for evidence. She's saved us a helluva lot of work by steering us away from one line of investigation and toward another. She takes the guesswork out of it, you understand?"

"So all she does is save you a little time and effort."

"Hey, don't sneer at that, man! And no, that isn't all she does.

Lotsa times we'd have missed out altogether if it wasn't for some lie she uncovered. And every time—*every* time—we got the evidence we needed. I'm telling you, she never misses."

"Never misses." *I'll take vanilla.*

"All right, believe it, don't believe it, what do I care? What do you want to do, read all the case records?"

"Yes," said Kevin Gilbert stubbornly.

"Eric," said Shelby, "I'll go with you to California, I'll live in California, I'll even pretend to like California. But don't ask me to give up my police work."

"Come on, Shelby, I'm not asking you to give up some career you've spent years preparing yourself for. This whole lie-detecting business—it's a fluke, and you know it. Is it worth breaking up our marriage for?"

"Would you ask me to stop singing if I happened to be born with a great voice? That's a fluke too."

"Not a valid analogy. Won't you even try it?"

"Try pretending I can't do something I can?"

"Maybe we can find some other way to use your gift, something that won't put you in the public eye."

"Like what?"

"Like I don't know what. But we can look for something. Or don't you think the marriage is worth the effort?"

Shelby was silent a moment. Then: "Yes, I think it's worth the effort. Oh hell, Eric—maybe you're right. I don't know, let me think about it some more. I don't want to give up the police work, but I don't want to give you up either. Why should I have to choose? It's not reasonable, what you're asking me to do."

"I know," he said gently. "But I'm still asking."

"Yes, Shelby was down last week," Dr. Wedner said. "We were running some new neurological tests. What is it exactly you want to know?"

"I want to know how reliable her ability is," Kevin Gilbert said.

"One hundred per cent," said Dr. Wedner. "You cannot tell her a lie without her knowing it, and she never mistakes the truth for a falsehood. She's foolproof. I've never tested another aura reader who even approaches Shelby in accuracy."

"You mean there are others like her?"

"There are other aura readers in the world, but none of them can read the same aura Shelby reads. She's the only one who can detect lies. But there are others who can spot physical illness by seeing auras the rest of us can't see. We've tested about a hundred of these people, and the mean for the group is sixty-four per cent accuracy. Still a long way from Shelby's perfect score."

"A policeman in New York told me that it was automatic," said Gilbert. "That she either saw a red glow or she didn't. How can that be? Truth and lies are usually mixed up together. How can it be a yes-or-no proposition?"

"Well, it's not exactly like that. Shelby sees gradations in the auras, different shades of red, depending on how much of what is being said is false. What you and I call white lies Shelby sees as pink. That's how it all started—when she entered adolescence she noticed her father glowing pink every once in a while. But the very nature of police investigation is such that the lies told the police are either bright red or dark red. That's what we're working on now—trying to figure out the difference between 'bright' and 'dark'."

"I suppose you have evidence to document all this."

"Tons of it," the scientist said unscientifically.

"Then I'd like to send in some people who are qualified to evaluate your testing program and its results. Do you have any objection?"

"None whatsoever," Dr. Wedner agreed cheerfully.

"Eric wants me to do *what?*" said Tee, appalled.

"He wants you to help him persuade Shelby to give up her police work," Max repeated.

"But I can't do that! That would . . . it would be downright *immoral* for Shelby to hide her talent! She . . . there's never been anyone like her, ever before! How could she . . . and he wants me to . . . she'd think I . . . I can't do it, Max!"

"Okay," he laughed.

"What?"

"I said okay. I think you're right."

"But you said—"

"I carried a message, Tee, that's all. We're going to have to let Shelby and Eric work it out for themselves."

"How many times have you consulted her?" asked Kevin Gilbert.

"Oh, nine or ten," said Lieutenant Nicolosi. "It'd be a lot more if she lived here in Pittsburgh, but we gotta pay air fare as well as her fee every time she comes. I tried to talk her into moving to Pittsburgh once, but she's got a husband who's tied to New York. Some sort of bigwig with the Jets."

Gilbert knew all about Eric Kent and his job. In fact, he'd learned almost everything there was to know about Shelby. "And she's never been wrong once?" he asked almost desultorily. "Not even once?"

"Not here she hasn't. She's been right on the money every time. Have you talked to the police in New York and Boston?"

"Yes." *And Philadelphia. And Detroit. And Atlanta. And everyplace else Shelby Kent and her extraordinary ability had added a new dimension to crime-fighting.*

"Anything else you want?" Lieutenant Nicolosi asked.

"No, I guess not," said Gilbert.

CHAPTER 15

PASTELS ARE CHEAPER

Winner of the Longest Song Title Contest: "Dear Okie, If You See Arkie, Tell Him Tex Has Got a Job for Him Out in Californy, Pickin' Up Prunes, Squeezin' Oil Out of Olives"

"We're all outa Cherries Jubilee," said the waiter.

"No you're not," Shelby smiled sweetly.

The waiter looked startled. "You calling me a liar?"

Eric spoke up. "The lady's saying you're mistaken. Cherries Jubilee. Care to try again?"

The waiter muttered something under his breath and trudged off to the kitchen.

"Now why would he lie about that?" asked Tee.

"Too much fuss," Max said. "Pulling the tray over here, lighting the cognac—extra effort for him."

"Terrific," sighed Tee.

"What's the matter, Tee?" Eric asked. "You look down in the dumps."

"Tchaikovsky," Tee mumbled.

"Tchaikovsky?"

Max said, "Metropolitan Ballet started rehearsing *The Nutcracker* today. The obligatory Christmas ritual for kids. Tee isn't exactly overjoyed."

Shelby smiled at her sister in sympathy.

"I sometimes wonder," Tee said, "whether children enjoy *The Nutcracker* as much as we like to think they do. It really is a boring ballet. Both to listen to and to watch. And I'm not altogether sure it's a wholesome thing for children to see. Here we have this rather peculiar little girl who has sexual fantasies about a, ahem, *nut*-cracker—a nutcracker that's been brought to her by an uncle who seems to be a sort of pander. In addition, the girl feels threatened by *mice!* So her way of coping with all this is to go dancing in the snow wearing nothing but a thin cotton nightgown. This child has problems."

"Why, Tee," laughed Shelby, "what a dreadful thing to say!"

"Tee doesn't like Tchaikovsky," Max explained unnecessarily.

"Hey, we're supposed to be celebrating, remember?" Eric poured more champagne. "To San Diego!"

Shelby lifted her glass dutifully. "Which we'll be calling 'home' exactly two months from tonight. To San Diego."

"Where I hope you'll both be very, very happy," Tee said earnestly.

"We will be," said Shelby. *Even if it kills us.*

"What are you going to be doing instead of police work?" Max asked Shelby.

Eric answered for her. "Dr. Wedner gave us the name of a man at Cal Tech. Maybe more tests, maybe something else. He'll find something for her to do."

"Something to keep the little woman busy," Shelby said.

"Now, Shel, you agreed," said Eric, annoyed at her tone.

"Yes, yes, I agreed."

"To sunny California," said Tee hastily, lifting an empty glass. "Where the skies are blue and the landscape is—"

"Beige," finished Shelby.

Eric forced a smile. "Ecru?" he said hopefully.

Max laughed. "That reminds me of a technical stage director I worked for once, when I was about nineteen." *Change the subject.* "Man named Ace, summer theater in Connecticut. Ace was shade blind. Not color blind—he could tell green from yellow and so on. But he couldn't distinguish among close shades of the same color. He couldn't tell beige from ecru, or even sky blue from aquamarine. He was still using the kind of scene paint that comes in powdered form that you mix with size water. Doesn't cost much that way. And Ace was a tight-fisted son of a gun—he never had us mix up any more paint than he thought we'd need. Which meant we often mixed up *less* than we needed, and then had to mix some more. So of course there was always the problem of making sure the shades matched exactly. Ace was always asking one of us if the new batch of paint matched the shade we'd already used. He pretended he was just checking to make sure, but he really couldn't see any difference at all.

"So one day when we'd just finished the flats for some musical we were doing, we were all standing around admiring our handiwork—airy, cheerful flats, all yellows and light greens and even some pinks, I think. Ace stood there for a minute and then said, 'One thing you have to say for this set, it sure is loud!' And in my usual tactful way I said, 'But Ace, they're all pastels!' Ace looked at me, and then looked at the flats, then looked at me again, then looked back at the flats. 'Well,' he said, 'pastels are cheaper!' And they are—dark shades cost more. But the man was so determined not to admit he couldn't tell the difference between 'loud' and 'pastel' that he pretended *economy* was the reason for his choice of colors."

Eric laughed politely while Tee played with her champagne glass; she'd heard all about Ace and his problems.

"Max," Shelby said quietly, "why did you tell that story? Something to do with false justification? Finding excuses for our bad choices?"

The table became ominously quiet.

Then: "Jesus Christ!" Eric exploded.

"I thought we were going to let them work it out by themselves," Tee said to her husband.

"I thought so too," Max said miserably. "Me and my big mouth."

"Cherries Jubilee," snarled the waiter.

CHAPTER 16

$34.50 STILL OWED
ON A GRECIAN URN

*The basic decisions on our participation in any conflict and
our response to any threat . . . will be made by the regularly
constituted civilian authorities.*

—John F. Kennedy, in an address
to Congress, 28 March 1961

. . . to bring you this special bulletin.

*Two near-simultaneous explosions have just taken the lives
of an estimated three thousand persons in Greece. One or more
bombs were detonated in the UN Militia Supply Headquarters
building in Athens an hour ago, destroying the building completely and injuring or killing its staff of over five hundred
workers as well as an undetermined number of passersby. The
headquarters co-ordinated supply movements for UN Militia installations in the entire eastern Mediterranean area.*

*Also bombed was a UN garrison outside Delvinakion, a small
town near the Greece–Albania border. Fatality estimates range
as high as twenty-five hundred. Early unconfirmed reports attrib-
ute the bombings to Greek guerrillas.*

*Stay tuned to this station for further details as they become
available.*

UN Special Commission Formed
To Investigate Terrorism

NEW YORK (AP)—The UN Security Council met in emergency session today to consider the problem of the recent unprovoked attacks on UN Militia installations.

Council members quickly agreed to the formation of a special commission of inquiry. Announcement of the membership of the commission and the extent of its investigatory powers is expected momentarily.

The commission's prime function is to inquire into the two bombings that took place in Greece two days ago. The death toll from those bombings has now reached 3,200.

Rumors about the formation of an investigating commission have been circulating ever since the aborted Honduran uprising in March. Neither the Honduran nor the earlier Burmese rebellion succeeded because the rebels in both countries had been supplied with defective weapons.

Pedro Yglesias, arrested as the supplier of the Honduran weapons, has implicated UN Ambassador Mañuel Aguirrez in a plot to support rebel uprisings.

EYES ONLY
TO: Sir John Dudley

Explosives used in Greek bombings were purchased from Franz Meier, a munitions distributor headquartered in Zürich. Meier's computer tapes of all purchasing records for the past six months have been erased. Meier is being held for further questioning.

No connection between the Greek bombings and Ambassador Mañuel Aguirrez has been uncovered.

But he doesn't know that, thought Sir John.

. . . in a bombshell announcement by Sir John Dudley, head of the UN Intelligence Agency. Sir John stated Ambassador Aguirrez has admitted responsibility for supplying Honduran rebels with defective arms but denies responsibility for the Greek bombings.

Sir John stated that Ambassador Aguirrez has displayed "deep distress" over the slaughter in Greece and is anxious to disclaim all personal responsibility.

Mr. Aguirrez named two other representatives to the UN as his "partners" in the business of supporting rebel groups in their activities against the UN Militia. The Ambassador says the bombings in Greece were the work of either Li Xijuan of the People's Republic of China or Heinrich Schlimmermann of West Germany.

The naming of Li Xijuan came as a special surprise. Ambassador Li served as chairwoman of the UN committee that drew up the organizational plans for both the Militia and its intelligence operation.

Ambassadors Aguirrez, Li, and Schlimmermann have been placed under diplomatic restraints pending the results of the UN special commission's investigation of the bombings in Greece and other rebel activities.

CHAPTER 17

CITIZEN KANE OR KILLER KANE?

The air had a nip in it; Sir John Dudley walked briskly through the park to get some of the cobwebs out of his head.

Mañuel Aguirrez, Li Xijuan, Heinrich Schlimmermann. The names didn't go together, had never been associated with one another before. They didn't even sound right together. Aguirrez, Li, Schlimmermann. In order of importance: Li, Schlimmermann, Aguirrez.

The real shocker was Li Xijuan. That small, quiet woman who'd shown herself to be a dynamo when it came to getting the Militia authorized, organized, and legalized. She'd led the fight for an international peacekeeping force and then had slave-driven her committee until it hammered out a workable plan. She'd survived criticism and setbacks, media attacks both overt and covert. And she'd triumphed over the worst enemy of all—wishywashyness among her peers. Some of her original supporters in the UN had begun to have second thoughts, and even back home the power structure had given her a bad moment: she was recalled to China. But she'd come back.

She'd come back and finished the job, and in the process had won over the doubting Thomases. Sir John was well acquainted with the power plays behind the formation of the Militia, and he'd marveled more than once at Li Xijuan's instinct for survival. She'd managed to convince the world—well, a sizable part of it—that the need for a strengthened and absolute international peacekeeping force was real and immediate. The growth of a world army was possible only through the diminishing of national armies. And Li Xijuan had made it happen. A remarkable woman.

So what was she doing mixed up with a political also-ran like Mañuel Aguirrez? For she was mixed up with him, no longer any question of that. Kevin Gilbert's staff had uncovered evidence of her attempt to engineer an illegal arms purchase through a dealer in Hong Kong. She'd wanted to buy a manufacturer-rejected batch of faulty laser-guided antitank missiles.

Which meant that Li Xijuan was undoubtedly the one who had arranged to supply the rebels in Burma with defective weapons. Which meant that she and Mañuel Aguirrez were in the rebellion-deflating business together. Which meant that she had sought *him* out—Aguirrez wasn't the type to initiate international intrigue. By his own admission.

The man was a baby. Sir John's interrogators had only to hint strongly that Aguirrez was going to be charged with the massacre in Greece when he broke down and started talking. It was all Li Xijuan's idea, he said. She'd come to him and to Heinrich Schlimmermann with this plan, see, a way to stop rebels from doing any serious damage. It was only for a while, she said, until the Militia could get itself solidly established. He didn't know what had gone wrong in Greece.

Sir John came to an empty park bench and sat down. Every year his legs seemed to tire a little more quickly than the year before—*I am an old man,* he thought. What had gone wrong in Greece, yes. Heinrich Schlimmermann was the only one of the improbable trio to make any sense. Schlimmermann was an aristocratic Aryan caught in an egalitarian society, and he'd risen to his present degree of eminence in part through sheer will, by keeping his arrogant streak beneath the surface, by learning to manipulate people. Heinrich Schlimmermann was used to getting his own way.

The explosives used in Greece had been obtained through a middleman in Zürich, a distributor whose purchasing records had conveniently been wiped out. That smacked of the much vaunted German efficiency, the near-obsessive desire to see that every little detail was taken care of. *Alles in Ordnung.* Bullshit, as the Americans would say. Sir John's years at Bletchley had taught him just how *in*efficient the Master Race could be.

But the Germans still liked to think of themselves as the most in-control people in the world. Like Heinrich Schlimmermann. He had all the requisite qualities: orderliness, aristocratic arrogance, a need to manipulate, a compulsion to power. Sir John strongly suspected that nothing had gone wrong in Greece. He suspected that Heinrich Schlimmermann had done exactly what he'd set out to do.

The upcoming UN inquiry, Sir John knew, would waste a lot of time on trying to determine motive. *Why* did you think this was the best way of handling insurrections, *why* did you do this or that. Let others worry about *why;* right now Sir John's responsibility was to determine *what.* By the time the inquiry officially opened, he would have enough hard evidence for the commission to nail these lethal meddlers in other people's lives.

But time was running short. Sir John had never seen a bureaucratic organization move as fast as the Security Council was moving now. The inquiry, fully televised, would begin in a matter of weeks. The membership of the commission was almost complete. The chairman hadn't yet been determined, but Sir John was betting on the Canadian. The American and Russian delegates were both on the commission, as were a couple of the Arab representatives—but nobody really trusted any of them. The other members of the commission were compromise choices, selected more for the geographical balance they offered than for their political influence. Sir John's money was on the Canadian.

He came to with a start. It was beginning to get dark—and here he was, sitting on his London derrière alone on a bench in perilous Central Park. Sir John hurried away as fast as his elderly legs would carry him.

CHAPTER 18

THE ONLY REBELLION LEFT

Shelby increased her pace as she rounded a corner onto Lexington Avenue and ducked into a storefront. There she hid behind a large woman with a shopping bag and pretended to stare intently at a window display of meerschaum pipes, all the while watching the street out of the corner of her eye.

There he was. The brown man hurried past without seeing her. Shelby slipped back into the stream of pedestrians behind him, determined to find out what he was up to. But she'd taken only a few steps when the man stopped abruptly and turned to look behind him. A big man, with brown hair, brown eyes.

"Here I am," Shelby said. "Now who the hell are you and why have you been following me?"

The man gave a half-laugh. "You're not supposed to find me out that easily."

"Is that meant to be disarming?" Shelby said suspiciously. "I want to know who you are."

"You know, you shouldn't just go up and accost strangers like that," he scolded. "Call a policeman, let him take care of it."

"Stop stalling. Show me some identification."

The brown man fished out a small leather folder. "My name's Gilbert. I'm with UN Intelligence," the man said, "and I wasn't following you, Mrs. Kent, so much as I was trying to catch up with you. I need to talk to you. It's important."

"You know my name."

"Could we talk? Now?"

"What's this all about, Mr. Gilbert? And don't try to lie to me—I'll know when you aren't telling the truth."

"I know," Gilbert sighed. "Oh boy do I know. Look, there's a fairly respectable-looking bar across the street—let's have a drink and I can explain everything."

The bar was half empty at midafternoon and they took a table in the corner. "Scotch straight up for me," Gilbert told the waitress, "and a Bourbon for the lady, no water, one ice cube." The waitress left, and Gilbert turned to find Shelby staring at him, mouth open. "Yes, we've been investigating you," he admitted. "Right down to what you like to drink. It's an atrocious invasion of privacy and how dare we and yes we've got our nerve. All I can say is that it was necessary. *Absolutely necessary.* We want you to come to work for us."

That wasn't what Shelby was expecting. "I don't know what to say."

"Don't say anything—let me talk. Ordinarily you'd be visited at home by a sedate group of two or three distinguished people who would make you a polite offer of employment mixed in with a little muscle if we thought that would help. But I wanted to meet you myself—I've learned things in my investigation that I still have trouble believing. When my boss first told me a human lie detector was living right here in New York, I thought the old boy was getting senile. I thought you were either a con woman or a figment of somebody's overactive imagination. But you're real, and you're here, and you're everything your reputation says you are. An absolutely foolproof detector of lies. Woman, you are worth your weight in gold."

"That much I know," Shelby said blandly. "Go on."

Gilbert said, "Li Xijuan, Mañuel Aguirrez, Heinrich Schlimmermann," and waited.

Shelby's eyes widened. "The UN commission of inquiry."

Gilbert nodded, and said nothing.

"You want me to sit in on your interrogation of Li Xijuan and the other two? To get evidence for the inquiry?"

"We want you to sit in *during* the inquiry. As part of the inquiry itself."

"Oh wow." Shelby thought a minute. "That's all going to be televised, isn't it?"

"That's right."

"Tell me how it would work."

"Well, Dr. Wedner tells me this aura you read can be photographed on specially modified infrared film but can't be transmitted live through any kind of optic lens—you have to see it in the flesh, isn't that right? That means we can't tuck you away in a private room somewhere and let you watch the proceedings over a monitor. You'll have to be in the chamber where the questioning takes place."

"And where the television cameras are set up."

"Yes," he said apologetically, knowing what was bothering her. "You won't have to speak at all, or identify yourself, or anything like that. We'll have some sort of electronic device rigged up so you can communicate with the members of the commission."

"But I'd still be visible."

"You'd still be visible."

Shelby shook her head and laughed. "You have a hell of a sense of timing, Mr. Gilbert. Another six weeks and I would have—but that's not your problem. Something I'm going to have to work out for myself."

"You mean the move to San Diego."

The waitress put their drinks on the table and left. "Is there anything about me you don't know?" Shelby asked with a touch of irritation.

"Very little. I know about the problem with your husband and I know you're worried about your sister. I know you don't want to leave New York or give up your police work, but you've made up your mind to do both."

"Those are private matters," Shelby said resentfully.

"I'm sorry. Would it help if I told you every one of us who works for UN Intelligence has been under the same microscope? Even Sir John Dudley himself."

"No, it doesn't help a bit."

"Then let me appeal to your sense of adventure. Why settle for nabbing petty crooks when you can go after international criminals? Mrs. Kent, this inquiry is too important for us to leave anything to chance. You're our ace in the hole. Let me make a suggestion. Simply postpone your move to San Diego. The inquiry won't last forever. And when it's over, we'll try to talk you into staying on and you can tell us all to go to hell if you like. But stay for the inquiry."

"It's not that simple."

"Nothing ever is." *Might as well bring it out in the open.* "Your husband won't like it."

"He'd never forgive me. He looks upon California as a place where he'd be free of the stigma of being married to a woman who knows every time he lies to her. But if I'm to be part of this inquiry, everybody in the world will know what I do. Eric'll be no better off in California than he is here. Oh, I know it all seems very petty to you—what's one marriage compared to what the Li Xijuan gang has been up to? But it's not petty to me. It's my life."

"I don't think it's petty at all."

Shelby smiled sadly. "You're not telling the truth, Mr. Gilbert."

Gilbert turned a different shade of red and then laughed. "I can see I'm going to have to be careful around you."

Shelby's smile disappeared. "Yes. Most people find it a terrible burden."

And with those simple words, Shelby made Kevin Gilbert see her in a totally new light. My God, yes—what must this woman feel like, knowing that other people regarded her as some kind of freak? Even the police who thought so highly of her ability looked on her as a sort of living machine to be plugged in for their convenience, never to be treated as a normal person. She *wasn't* normal—but in only one way. In all other respects she was just a human being, one who must surely be sensitive to the waves of resentment her gift provoked. Maybe that was why she was willing to give up everything for a husband who was giving her only a hard time in return. Maybe Eric Kent was the best she could hope for.

"I thought I knew so much about you," Gilbert said. "I'm beginning to think I know nothing at all."

Shelby looked at him curiously, wondering what he meant. "When does the inquiry start?"

"The date hasn't been announced yet, but it'll be about two weeks from now. They have to move fast. The Security Council's trying to put down the fear that some kind of worldwide rebellion is in the works. A lot of folks think these attacks on the Militia are all part of a unified drive by person or persons unknown to take over the world."

"And you're sure they aren't?" Shelby asked dubiously.

"Positive. Li Xijuan and Aguirrez and Schlimmermann have simply been exploiting disparate groups of malcontents for their own cloudy purposes. Remember Li and Aguirrez supplied *their* rebels with guns that wouldn't shoot and bombs that wouldn't explode. Schlimmermann broke the pattern when he took it on himself to blow up three thousand people in Greece."

"I notice you say rebels instead of revolutionaries. A way of diminishing them?"

"Yes, it's deliberate, I admit. Revolution has become so commonplace the word has almost lost its meaning. I went to Honduras, I talked to those people. They don't want to establish a new social order—they haven't thought that far. They just want to hit out at something, enlarge themselves at the expense of other people's lives. And *they* are the sort of people Li Xijuan and her two partners-in-crime have been seeking out. Excitable people, easily stirred up. What those three have been doing is ugly, ugly as hell, and it has to be aired publicly. And fast. So what I want most in the world is to hear a big, resounding *yes* from you right now."

"But you don't really expect to hear it, do you?" Shelby grinned.

"Of course I do," Gilbert said stoutly, glowing red.

"Saying yes to you would change my entire life. I'm not sure I want to change my entire life."

"Look, Shelby, I don't want to tell you—oh, I'm sorry. Mrs. Kent."

"Shelby's okay. What's your first name?"

"Kevin."

"Then fire away, Kevin. Go ahead and don't tell me what you don't want to tell me."

"I don't want to tell you how to make personal decisions, but for the life of me I can't see how you could consider *not* taking the job! This inquiry may be *the* event of the century—"

"More than two world wars, space flight, cloning . . ."

"—and here you have the chance to play a vital part in it! I'd jump at the chance, myself. It's *big*." He reached out and took her hand. "Shelby, it's bigger than both of us."

She burst out laughing and withdrew her hand. "You're very good at your job, Kevin Gilbert. But I can't make a decision just like that." She tried to snap her fingers and failed. "I'll need some time to think about it."

She didn't say no, she said she'd think about it! Let it percolate. "Time you shall have. Meet me here tomorrow at three o'clock and tell me your decision."

"Gee, that's almost twenty-four hours. Sure you can wait that long?"

"Actually, no. I'd say I don't want to rush you, but you'd know I was lying. I do want to rush you. But I can't force you. If you haven't reached a decision by tomorrow, you can tell me here and we'll arrange to meet the next day. How else can I get away with dating a married woman? But I'd rather have you put me off than tell me no. Think about it very carefully."

"I will." Shelby smiled.

Kevin Gilbert signaled the waitress. "Let's have another drink and talk about something else. Two more," to the waitress. "Tell me about your sister's name."

"Tee?"

"Tee. Her name's Martita, why don't you call her Marty?"

"As far as that goes, why don't we call her Martita? It's a perfectly good name." Shelby shrugged. "I don't know, she's always been called Tee. The strong syllable in Martita."

"That's as good a reason as any." The waitress was back with their refills. "She used to be a pianist, didn't she?"

"Lord, what an awful way of putting it. Used to be. Remember the old poser—is a play still a play without an audience? Is a pianist a pianist if nobody hears the music? Tee still plays, hours and hours every day. But she won't give concerts."

"Why not?"

"Scared. Tee doesn't have the right personality for coping with hordes of people pushing at her. She doesn't even like to go out of her apartment any more than she has to. She . . . she's a very private person, Kevin. It's hard to explain. She has this extraordinary talent—really extraordinary. She ought to be out there conquering the world! But putting herself on display is painful to her, a breach of some kind of decorum that's important to her. Every time she's performed in public she's been in agony."

"Stage fright?"

"No, I don't think so. Tee is a very poised musician, incredibly so . . . do you know what she did? She won the Three Rivers Piano Competition when she was only sixteen years old—all the other contestants were in their late twenties, thereabouts. And she won with Prokofieff's *First Piano Concerto*. Do you know the Prokofieff? You have to have fingers of steel to play that one! And Tee did it. Sixteen years old, and she did it. I was so proud of her I felt I was going to burst. She went on to give concerts and make a few guest appearances with symphony orchestras. She even recorded some Bach on the London label. But then she started finding excuses not to accept this engagement, not to go on that tour. Her public appearances grew farther and farther apart, and eventually stopped altogether. Now she works part time as a rehearsal pianist for some third-rate ballet company, and she wouldn't even be doing that if it weren't for Max's encouraging her to get out and do *something*. Max is her husband."

"I know."

"Oh yes, of course you do, I forgot. Max has turned out to be a real jewel. He knows how to nudge instead of shove, and he's patience personified. I think Tee would have settled into a *hausfrau* role long ago if it hadn't been for Max and why am I telling you all this?" Shelby suddenly looked appalled. "I don't even know you, and here I am talking about private family matters . . ."

Kevin smiled reassuringly. "Happens in Russian novels all the time. Don't be embarrassed, Shelby—this is a private conversation between you and me. I'm not going to rush back and feed what you've said into the computer."

"I hope not." She *was* embarrassed. "Kevin, you're a great listener, but I'd like to end the conversation now."

"Of course." He put some money on the table and stood up. As they were about to go out through the door, he touched her arm. "Shelby, all kidding aside, we need you badly. This inquiry *is* big—and it's serious. Deadly serious."

"I know," Shelby said with a shudder.

CHAPTER 19

DIOGENES REMEMBERED

He looked like one of those men the Americans were always "retiring" to Sicily, thought Sir John Dudley, but he was on the verge of becoming a symbol for the world's perennial battle against lawlessness.

P. J. Martel pushed himself to his feet, a huge mountain of a man, and lumbered toward his visitor with his hand outstretched. "Thank you for coming, Sir John. Take that chair—it's the most comfortable."

The entire office looked comfortable. Sir John murmured something as he shook hands and lowered himself into the indicated chair. This would be their last conference before the inquiry officially opened.

"One last-minute change," Martel said. "Originally we'd planned to save Li Xijuan until last, but we've decided to sandwich her in between the other two. That means her staff and associates will be under scrutiny a little earlier than we'd planned. That won't cause your office any difficulty, will it?"

"No, their dossiers are fairly full right now. We'll keep looking for evidence, of course, but I'm sure you already have enough there to indict."

"Good, good. Whichever way this inquiry goes, it's going to be a precedent-setter. The old definitions of treason won't work in a United Nations tribunal. So if we vote to send all three of them before a tribunal, we'd better be damned sure of what we're doing. It's going to be a long haul—miles to go before we sleep. But I think we're ready."

Sir John thought so too. And he felt a cautious confidence in this big Canadian's ability to handle the presentation of evidence properly. P. J. Martel was not a young man, but he had reserves of energy Sir John frankly envied. And Martel was a *law*-man, in the most literal sense of the word.

"I met your Mrs. Kent yesterday." Martel chuckled. "Very direct, isn't she? I have something to confess, Sir John. I plowed through that mountain of scientific data from Rutgers University, I read all the police reports, I talked at great length with Kevin Gilbert. I had to accept the evidence—Shelby Kent is indeed a woman who can unerringly tell the difference between factual truth and deliberate falsehood."

"No question."

"But the whole idea of a human lie detector was so strange that I still found a lingering trace of skepticism in myself—in spite of all that evidence. So when she came here yesterday I almost unconsciously started slipping little falsehoods into the conversation—wanting to trip her up, you see. The first couple of times she looked at me oddly but said nothing. The third time, she said, 'Excuse me, is this some sort of test or am I supposed to ignore all these lies you're telling?'" The Canadian laughed. "My secretary was shocked."

"I've never met Mrs. Kent myself," Sir John said. "Gilbert made the contact."

Martel wagged his big head. "I can't get over our good fortune in having her. Has there ever before been an investigation in which conflicting testimony could be so readily resolved?"

"We're fortunate to have her in more ways than one. Her helping us involves some personal sacrifice." Sir John didn't elaborate. "We couldn't force her to co-operate. *She* could lie to *us* if she wanted to and we'd have no way of checking up on her. Not until someone else comes along who can read that same aura."

Martel was nodding. "Perhaps it's just as well she has no legal status—forces us to depend solely on external evidence. And that's as it should be. 'Advisory capacity only.' That's how the publicity releases will read."

"About that," said Sir John. "Could you hold off making any announcement? I understand she wishes to avoid publicity as much as possible."

"But of course. However, it's not going to be possible to conceal her function for long. Sooner or later the newshawks are going to get wind of it."

"Then let's try for later. Give her as much anonymity as you can for as long as you can."

"Whatever the lady wants," Martel said agreeably. "Did I tell you we've decided not to call Martinez? The man's obviously just hired muscle and knows nothing about the conspiracy."

"Yes, you're right there. You are still starting with Aguirrez's people, aren't you?"

"Attack the weak link first, that's the ticket. Pedro Yglesias will be up first."

Sir John permitted a small smile. "You'll be inundated with slogans, you know."

Martel smiled back. " 'Down with the tyrants,' that sort of thing? One might as well take out an ad in the New York *Times* saying 'Be nice.' These shibboleths never change much, do they? Both vague and inflammatory, a slogan for all seasons."

Sir John nodded, remembering other slogans from other times. *V* for Victory. The Final Solution. Make Love, Not War. In a literal sense, too generalized to mean anything much. But in the context of their origins—repositories of hopes and hatreds and anxieties intense enough to sway millions. Martel was right. Sloganeering never changed much.

CHAPTER 20

TAKE A DEEP BREATH
AND COUNT TEN

Shelby Kent sat stiffly in a more-for-show chair, aware of, annoyed by, the occasional furtive glance directed her way. Who she was and why she was there: supposedly a secret. A secret like all other government secrets—carefully leaked to selected sympathetic investigators from the communications media. Whose numbers were legion.

The antechamber prickled with a perpetual coming and going of people looking busy, some truly busy. Kevin Gilbert stood beside her chair and slightly in front of her, not hiding her but announcing through his posture that Shelby was not accessible to just anyone who cared to stop and chat. He'd been riding shotgun for her ever since she arrived, fending off questioners, showing her quick ways out of the hearing chamber, showing her back exits from the building. But he could do nothing about the glare of camera lights aimed in her direction. *Smile?*

Too much authority here. Member A spoke for umpty million people, Member B for umpty-plus. And there were Members C through Z and a couple of alphabets more. *The world,* thought Shelby, *the whole world is right here, passing through this determinedly modern, aesthetically boring antechamber in the UN Building. Today we make history.*

The carefully cultivated image of power and authority was doing its job. *Shelby's hands are all sweaty, Miz Williams*—a voice from the past, a smirking classmate exposing Shelby's weakness to her peers. Grown-up, worldly, experienced Shelby Kent ran her hands down her thighs. *Dry, damn you, DRY.*

Kevin Gilbert's hand (dry) against her arm: Shelby rose and made her way toward the hearing chamber. They had decided to put her back of the main table among Chairman P. J. Martel's cadre of note-takers, errand-runners, advisers, process-servers, statute-checkers, lookers-up-of-analogies. A crowd easy to get lost in. Kevin pointed to a more-for-comfort chair, and Shelby sat. A lawyer on one side of her, a woman who didn't speak English on the other. To her immediate right was The Machine.

A simple machine. One row of twenty-one lights and two buttons. Each of the lights was labeled with the name of one of the ambassadors on the commission. If one of them wished Shelby's judgment, he or she would press a button in an ordinary communications outlet, flashing the corresponding light on The Machine. In answer Shelby would press one of *her* two buttons—*Yes, No.*

The Canadian-born chairman of the commission was making an opening statement alternately in English and French, droning on about integrity and co-operation among all peoples. From where Shelby sat he looked something like a walrus. Gross body, drooping mustaches, three chins, coarse skin. Definitely a walrus. Over seventy, but hair as black as coal. Dyed?

Red light, camera lens aimed at her. Somewhere in a sound-proofed room a well-groomed actor was sitting, reading out facts about her private life that his network's research staff had dug up. Was Eric watching? *Don't watch, Eric.*

The walrus had finished his statement and there was a brief pause as Pedro Yglesias was led into the hearing chamber. Shelby picked up her earphone and fitted it in place; Yglesias would be questioned in Spanish. Another *Untermensch*: Yglesias had the same look as the Loser in Pittsburgh, trying to act defiant when he really wanted to cringe.

The questioning began and immediately Shelby was in trouble. The translator's voice coming through her earphone was slurred, hard to follow. (*Dame Edith Evans' comment on the then-new generation of actors: "Poor dears, they have no vowels."*) Shelby didn't have to understand what was being said to tell whether Yglesias was lying or not, but dammit, she wanted to know what was going on! She looked around for Kevin Gilbert and signaled him with her eyes. Immediately he was at her side, and she whispered to him what was wrong. He nodded and left the chamber; fifteen minutes later a new voice spoke in her ear—veddy crisp, veddy British.

One of the commissioners was taking Yglesias through a step-by-step account of all his munitions-distributing activities. Where he shipped from. Methods of shipment. Receivers of the shipments. Names, places, dates. Shelby glanced at Martel: talking to one of his aides, paying no attention to Yglesias. The Mexican named names all morning until the lunch break was called.

"Nobody's signaled me even once," Shelby complained to Kevin Gilbert over lunch. "Have they forgotten I'm there?"

"They don't need to check up on Yglesias," Kevin explained. "They already have all the answers to the questions they're asking. This is just nuts-and-bolts stuff for the record, Shelby. All they're doing now is laying a legal foundation for the real questioning that comes later. Didn't Martel explain this to you?"

Shelby shook her head. "From my one interview with him, I got the impression he didn't want me to know *anything*. Wants me to go in cold, I suppose."

After lunch: more nuts-and-bolts questions, stretching on until four o'clock. Then, when even the most persnickety of the commissioners had been satisfied, the questioning left the arena of Yglesias's provable activities and ventured into the nebulous world of *why*.

"To fight tyranny," Pedro Yglesias said defiantly.

"Do you mean the UN Militia is made up of tyrants?" asked the Algerian commissioner.

"I do not know."

"Or perhaps that the Militia is keeping tyrants in power?"

"Perhaps, perhaps not. I do not know."

"If you do not know, how can you be sure you are indeed fighting tyranny?"

"I trust my leader. And," Yglesias boasted, "I know how to follow orders."

Here it was.

"Who is your leader, Señor Yglesias?"

"Señor Mañuel Aguirrez, Ambassador to the United Nations from the glorious republic of Mexico."

Meh-hee-co. So Aguirrez's name was in the official records for the first time.

The questioning then concentrated on contacts between Yglesias and his "leader," how his instructions were conveyed, what those instructions were. It was half an hour later before Chairman Martel asked, "Did you know the weapons you were shipping were defective?"

"No, sir, I did not."

There it was: a light pink glow, very faint, but definitely there. Shelby glanced at her machine—only one light lit. Martel's.

She signaled *No*.

The walrus bore in hard on Yglesias, and soon the frightened Mexican was contradicting himself, retracting. The story came out: Yglesias had "borrowed" a handgun from the Harlem warehouse arsenal and later found it wouldn't fire. He then "borrowed" a second gun and found that one wouldn't fire either. So he began to *suspect* there was something funny about the shipment but no sir he didn't really *know* they were all defective it wasn't his job to check them just to ship them sir.

Every light on Shelby's machine lit up. Unhesitatingly she hit the *Yes* button: this time the man was telling the truth.

Eight count them eight television cameras now pointing at Shelby Kent. She'd been a fool to think she could stay out of the limelight.

CHAPTER 21

INVITATION TO SMALLNESS

Test Your Ability in Syllogistic Reasoning

MAJOR PREMISE: Hard work is honorable.
MINOR PREMISE: Stealing refrigerators is hard work.
CONCLUSION:

"So much for anonymity," Eric said sourly.

"Yes, it was a foolish idea." She was tired. Only the first day, and already she was tired.

"What if you don't go back?"

"I don't think they'll let me not go back."

"Bull. We can get on a plane tonight and be on the other side of the country by the time they convene tomorrow morning. What are they going to do, postpone the inquiry until an armed guard can come get you?"

Shelby smiled and didn't answer. They'd been through this so many times. In three weeks Eric was scheduled to leave for San Diego, where Shelby would join him as soon as the commission no longer needed her services. And until the inquiry was over, one or the other of them would make the cross-country flight every Friday night; Shelby had convinced her husband that a weekend marriage would be good for both of them for a while.

"Look, Shel, it was all right at first, when you were just sitting in on police interrogations here in town. That was local, confined—still in the family, so to speak. It was even all right when police agencies outside New York started asking for you," Eric said, glowing pinkly.

"Why, thank you," said Shelby. *How generous of you.*

"Don't be sarcastic, please, Shelby. You know as well as I that this thing has gotten out of hand. Have you looked outside the building?"

Shelby knew what was out there. Mobile units and cameras and cables and sight-destroying lights and earnest young people talking earnestly into microphones. Price of notoriety.

Say something soothing. "It'll pass—the novelty will wear off. Something else will come along to distract them."

"You know it's not just them." Eric sat down tensely on the edge of a chair. Ready to spring and attack.

"Buck and Hubbs again?"

"Everybody. Thank God this is my last week with the Jets—I don't think I can take much more. People I thought were friends or at least friendly seem to be getting a hell of a kick out of my predicament."

"Your *predicament!*"

"That's what I said. 'Compulsory fidelity,' one of them called it."

"And you accept that standard? That a man is somehow less of a man if he doesn't cheat on his wife?"

"Don't be naïve, Shelby. How far do you think I'm going to get in San Diego if I'm an object of fun to my co-workers out there as well? Can't you understand what it's like?"

"I think I can," said Shelby, "and I'm truly sorry those clowns you work with are making you feel humiliated. And I'm even sorrier you're letting them do it."

"How can I stop them? You—"

"No, I mean you should be ashamed of *them* instead of me."

Eric grunted and didn't answer.

No lovemaking that night.

CHAPTER 22

WARTS AND ALL

Bored with listening to the same testimony over and over, Shelby turned down the volume of her earphone and just stared at the crowd of actors in this international Perry Mason show. Raised voice and flexed muscle—the UN's predictable response to any threat to its still new Militia. Like Creon, whose very first edict as king was violated by the young Antigone. Intraglobal hemistichs bounding back and forth throughout the hearing chamber.

By the end of the week the commission had finished questioning Mañuel Aguirrez's associates and were ready to start in on Aguirrez himself. Then the commission decided that all three of the about-to-be-accused should be present in the hearing chamber for the rest of the inquiry.

The Parade of the World-Shapers. Accusees Numbers One, Two, and Three—Teutonic, Latin, Oriental. (*Once there were a German, a Mexican, and a Chinaman who had to cross a river in a two-man boat . . .*) All the news media had been quick to point out that the rebels the three had "assisted" lived in sections of the world where nationalistic feelings ran high. The UN openly advocated a policy of "reasonable ethnicity": keeping some national identity, it was thought, would help mollify those who feared the impersonality of the global government toward which the world was clearly heading. So nationalist groups all over the world met regularly to complain, sing songs, wear uniforms, go home happy. Great unions from little catharses grow.

Three little conspirators sitting in a row. Li Xijuan in the center—small, poised, an almost-smile touching her lips. A Mona Lisa-Mata Hari whose face was the most familiar of the three. To her left, Mañuel Aguirrez—head lowered, body slumped in textbook posture of defeat. To Li Xijuan's right, Heinrich Schlimmermann—unfocused eyes, unmoving lips: inscrutable Occidental.

P. J. Martel was questioning Aguirrez. Yes, Aguirrez said, he had authorized the illegal shipment of arms to Honduras. Yes, he knew the defective weapons would lead to the deaths of the rebels. Yes, he had known he would eventually be found out. Occasionally a light would flash on Shelby's machine. *Yes, Yes, Yes.* Nothing but the truth.

Martel paused, looking more like a walrus than ever. "Ambassador Aguirrez," said the walrus, "will you tell us why in the name of heaven you ordered faulty weapons supplied to the Honduran rebels?"

Aguirrez lost his dead, defeated look for the first time since he'd entered the hearing chamber. His head lifted. A shaky right hand began to raise itself. (*He's alive, Colin Clive, he's alive!*) Aguirrez used the hand to steady himself as he rose from his chair.

"For you," said Aguirrez. "I do this thing for you!"

All the extraneous noise in the chamber died down. "Say again?" came a voice from somewhere.

"I do this thing for you!" Aguirrez shouted. "For you, for me, for all of us! For the United Nations! I help the United Nations!"

Holy frijoles. Shelby ignored her flashing machine momentarily while she studied the excited man carefully. No doubt about it. She pressed *Yes.*

A murmur ran all the way down the commissioners' table. Shelby saw the walrus lean back and say something to an aide. The aide jumped up and hurried toward Shelby.

She anticipated the question. "The machine did not malfunction—I signaled *Yes.* As far as Aguirrez knows, he's telling the truth. He's sincerely convinced he was helping the UN."

Scuttle back, tell the boss, pass the word. Mutter, mumble. Quiet, please: the show must go on.

"Ambassador, how does supplying rebels with faulty weapons help the UN?"

"If the weapons don't work, they cannot hurt the Militia, yes? And if the Militia is strong, the UN is strong. The Hondurans had been agitating for over a year, and yet no one was doing anything about it!"

"Because they weren't armed, Ambassador. They made a lot of

noise, but they were a threat to no one. By putting weapons in their hands—weapons which the rebels didn't know were useless—you provoked the very sort of incident the Militia is supposed to *prevent*."

Aguirrez grew agitated. "They had to be stopped—*someone* had to do something!"

"No sir, someone did *not* have to do something." The walrus pawed through some papers until he found what he wanted. "Ambassador, I have here a list of casualties provided by the Militia. According to our count, five hundred ninety Honduran rebels were killed and eighty wounded, two Militia dead and one wounded, twenty-three non-rebelling villagers dead—four of whom were children. That's a total of six hundred fifteen people who are dead because you took unilateral action to, ah, *correct* a situation that was already under control." Then, shrewdly: "Whose idea was this?"

Aguirrez closed his eyes for a moment and took a deep breath. "I am responsible for arming the Honduran rebels," he maintained. "I alone. You may not understand, but history will judge me right! I do not regret what I have done, even if I die for it."

The walrus looked pained at the other man's melodramatics but merely said, "Did someone approach you with a plan for strengthening the Militia by providing its enemies with inoperative weapons?"

Aguirrez had already implicated Li Xijuan in the pre-inquiry questioning, so he said, "Yes, the Ambassador from the People's Republic of China." The woman's face remained a mask.

Li Xijuan's name was now in the record.

Aguirrez became confused and incoherent under further questioning. It was clear to Shelby that the man didn't really understand that the arbitrary violence he'd made possible hadn't helped anybody. But that didn't make any difference to Aguirrez. Hero, martyr, defender of his fellow man! That was how he saw himself. Understanding was less important than wholehearted conviction.

And Mañuel Aguirrez was just bursting with conviction.

CHAPTER 23

YES, SANTA CLAUS,
THERE IS A VIRGINIA

Q. Over six hundred deaths resulted from the Honduras rebellion for which Mañuel Aguirrez authorized the shipment of arms, even though the rebels earlier posed no serious threat. And yet you signaled the commissioners that Aguirrez was telling the truth when he said he was helping the UN. Could you explain that to our viewing audience?

A. If you mean can I explain Aguirrez's line of reasoning, no, I can't. I'm not a mind reader, remember. What I can do is tell whether someone is lying or not. Aguirrez *believed* he was helping the UN. He *believed* the rebels were dangerous. Therefore, he was telling the truth.

Q. So all truth is relative?

A. Hardly. But one man's "truth" depends upon the limits of his own understanding. All I can say is that Aguirrez was not deliberately lying.

Q. But six hundred people are dead because of him. To call this "helping" the UN is slightly ridiculous, wouldn't you say?

A. I'd say it's more than ridiculous. I'd call it ugly and horrible and insane. But my opinion doesn't matter. It's *Aguirrez's* truth that's being questioned.

Q. Is it true that your testimony is inadmissable in a court of law?

A. Yes. That's why I never testify.

Q. Yet you influence the commissioners in their line of questioning?

A. I am here in an advisory capacity, to be consulted or ignored at the commissioners' discretion.

Q. But they all depend on that little machine of yours, don't they? I've noticed some of the commissioners never move their hands away from their signal button.

A. How very observant of you.

Q. Do you think it's quite ethical that someone with no legal standing should control an inquiry of this magnitude?

A. I don't control the inquiry! What an absurd idea.

Q. Is it? Isn't it true that the questions would most likely take a different tack if you weren't present?

A. You could say that of everyone who's participating in these proceedings. I'm merely one part of a large organization. I don't even know ahead of time what questions are going to be—

Q. Surely you don't claim your part in all this is just like everyone else's?

A. Oh, no. My part is quite different. Not more, or better—just different. That's why you keep thrusting that microphone under my nose every time you see me. My differentness. It makes a story for you.

Q. More than that. We're all deeply concerned about the legal and ethical implications of using your services.

A. You're lying.

CHAPTER 24

LIKE NIOBE, ALL TEARS

"Kind of rough today, wasn't it?" Eric said.

"Is that a chortle I hear in your voice?"

"Well, Shelby, when you push yourself into the public eye, you've got to expect things like that."

When you push yourself. "I've not 'got' to expect *anything.*" Shelby dropped into a chair and kicked off her shoes. "What I'd like to expect is a little understanding and support from my loving husband."

Eric smiled tightly. "Sorry, didn't mean to rub it in. Tee called—wants us to come to dinner. Feel up to it?"

"Did she sound nervous?"

"No, she was very cheerful."

"Then let's go. I could do with a spot of cheer."

Tee Bradley, nee Martita Fleming, formerly *pianiste extraordinaire*, now would-be housewife, valiantly fought the battle of middle cuisine to, at best, a draw. *If you can read, you can cook,* the saying went. Tee believed that. She really did. And she tried.

"The artichoke is delicious," Max lied.

"You like it?" asked Tee.

"Yes, indeed. Let's have 'em again soon."

Shelby sipped at her wine to hide a smile. How Tee had managed to ruin four perfectly good artichokes was a mystery—they were so *easy.* Nice Max, with his kind lies.

"The steaks are even better," Eric offered.

Tee smiled bravely. "Max did the steaks."

Shelby laughed an easy laugh. "Tee, you know Eric is a meatatarian. Next time give him a plate of raw beef and save the artichokes for Max and me."

Tee beamed.

"What happens next?" Max asked Shelby.

"Li Xijuan is up. I think they've decided Aguirrez is a dead end."

"Li Xijuan? I'd have thought they'd go after Schlimmermann next. Li Xijuan has always struck me as being . . . inaccessible."

"The commissioners probably think so too. I got the impression they're saving Schlimmermann for last in case they strike out with Li Xijuan."

"Aiming for a strong finish?"

"I guess."

"That's politics for you." Max laughed. "Just like show biz."

"The whole thing's show biz," said Eric. "Far too public."

Shelby groaned.

Tee said: "I think you were too polite to that creep who interviewed you today. You should have just brushed him off once he started on that ethics business."

Oh, Tee, you're not the one to tell me how to stand up to people!

"I've been instructed to co-operate with the news media at all times," Shelby said aloud. "To help compensate for the bungled attempt at keeping my function secret at first."

"Co-operate, yes. But that doesn't mean you have to put up with abuse."

"He wasn't abusive—just impertinent. Straw in the wind, though. It'll probably get worse."

"Oh?" said Eric, slowly putting down his fork.

"That's what I'm told." When Eric didn't say anything, she went on: "Better be prepared for it, Eric."

Hands on the table, chair back, Eric gone.

The Bradleys stared at Shelby and then at each other, not knowing what to say. Shelby broke the silence. "I think Eric's just about reached his breaking point."

Tee's eyes filled with tears. "What are you going to do?"

"Not much I can do, now. Eric's plan of starting over fresh in San Diego—well, that's shot to hell. All this publicity. He'll go out to California preceded by his reputation as the husband of a freak."

"Oh, Shelby, I'm sure Eric doesn't think you're a freak," Max said, concerned.

"You're glowing, Max."

"Aw, Shelby." Tee sniffled.

"Maybe it's my fault," Shelby said. "Maybe I just expected too much of him, wanted him to be bigger than I had any right to expect. Everybody lies. *Everybody*. Stop crying, Tee. Ironic, isn't it? Eric earns a good living by spreading the word, but when he tries to keep something quiet—well, it turns around and works against him."

Max looked glum. "You can't keep your talent secret."

"Maybe it really is just too much to live with," Shelby said. "Would you two be so blissfully happy if one of you knew every time the other was lying?"

"We don't lie to each other," Tee objected.

"You might not think so, but you do. You can't help it. But where's the dividing line between white lies and the nasty kind? Why should truth be so . . . so *harmful?*"

"Ibsen had a few things to say about that." Max smiled. "He didn't have any hard-and-fast answers either. Shelby, it's out of your hands now. You're going to have to leave it up to Eric."

"That's what worries me," said Shelby.

CHAPTER 25

TERENCE, IT'S *ALL*
STUPID STUFF

Once there was a king of a tribe in Africa who was greatly loved by his people. To show their respect and admiration, the people built him a magnificent throne of solid gold. The king sat on his solid gold throne beneath the jungle trees, and his fame spread throughout the world.

People came from everywhere to see this magnificent throne and the man for whom it was built. National Geographic *printed a two-part article. WNET sent in a camera crew, accompanied by two bearded young men asking for pledges. The people of the tribe were happy, seeing the importance of their beloved king.*

But at last the long African summer came to an end, and the rainy season began. When the king's throne was moved into his hut, there was very little room left for the king and his family. So the king's people built a huge shelf in the hut, a sort of second ceiling. The throne was placed on the shelf and everyone was happy. But that night the shelf collapsed— the throne fell upon the king and his family and killed them all.

Moral: People who live in grass houses shouldn't stow thrones.

The primate sitting opposite Shelby had been assigned to do an in-depth interview of the world's only living lie detector.

"Do you have any pet peeves?" asked the primate.

" 'The world is so full of lamentable things,' " Shelby misquoted, " 'I'm sure we should all be as miserable as kings.' "

"Whazzat?"

"Nothing. Yes, I have some pet peeves. Magazine inserts. The cheap glue the postal service puts on stamps. People who say *different than*."

"Different than what?"

Shelby just looked at him.

The primate made a gesture that might have been a shrug and asked, "Who does your hair?"

"Who—? Oh, for crying out loud. I do my own hair."

"What's your favorite recipe?"

Shelby gnashed her teeth. "Boiled water."

"Boiled water?"

"It helps stimulate the circulation of the blood." Shelby looked on with amazement as the primate dutifully wrote this down.

"How do you solve your sexual problems?"

"By consulting *The Aeneid* for advice."

"How d'you spell that?"

Shelby spelled it for him. "Look, aren't you going to ask me anything about my ability to detect lies?"

The primate looked bored. "If you like."

"Well, for the past four years I've been participating in a testing program at Rutgers—"

"What's your favorite television program?"

"*Screw the Press*," said Shelby.

"Mrs. Kent," coughed the walrus, "since I'm in charge of this circus, I must ask you to treat the communications media with a little more caution." *Hack, hack.* "Stick to neutral, noncommittal answers. It's safer."

"Have a cough drop," said Shelby.

P. J. Martel accepted a medicinal candy but refused to be side-tracked. "We need their good will, you know. They do a lot of our investigating for us. Always have done."

"What's the P.J. stand for?" Shelby asked idly.

"Pajamas," the walrus deadpanned. "Now pay attention. Neither you nor I nor any of us can afford the luxury of telling the communications media where to get off. We need those people—this inquiry is just too delicate for us to risk alienating the press."

"Have *you* ever been asked what your favorite recipe is?"

"I didn't say it was easy. But you must show respect for the press, Mrs. Kent."

"But I do," Shelby deadpanned in her turn. "I show them every bit as much respect as they show me."

The walrus hack-laughed. "Now I'm not asking you, Mrs. Kent, I'm telling you—watch what you say in future."

"Oh, all right," Shelby sighed. "I'll watch it."

"Good." *Hackety-hack.*

CHAPTER 26

SIMONE SIMON SAYS

. . . a riddle wrapped up in an enigma inside a mystery.

—Spoken of Russia by Winston Churchill,
who never met Li Xijuan

Li Xijuan turned her almost-smile toward the walrus. "Yes, I support the United Nations. I do not advocate its overthrow."

Yes, signaled Shelby.

The walrus thought for a moment. "Do you support the United Nations as it is presently constituted?"

Was that a smile? "But naturally."

Again, *Yes.* Li Xijuan was telling the truth.

The commission had spent seven days questioning the Chinese Ambassador's subordinates and associates, various bankers, shipping clerks, and truck drivers, and a few Burmese religious leaders. Proved beyond doubt was Li Xijuan's involvement in the useless weapons industry. She'd made it possible for the Burmese fanatics to create the circumstances of their own destruction. She'd later tried to purchase defective antitank missiles in Hong Kong. And UN Intelligence had just turned up evidence that Li Xijuan had been planning a raid on an arms factory in her own homeland—a factory with a low production record owing to the large number of weapons that had to be discarded because of some flaw in their manufacture.

The woman was guilty, all right. Guilty as hell.

"May I remind my fellow delegates," the Oriental woman was saying, "that I was one of the architects of the UN Militia? It has been my purpose to support the UN and all its branches—to help, not to hurt." She came even closer to smiling. "And I intend to do everything in my power to see that the Militia works."

"How does arming hostile people accomplish that?"

"It doesn't."

"Then why—?"

"A mistake, sir."

Shelby stared incredulously. As clear as anything: an unmistakable red aura around Li Xijuan's body. She hit the *No* button, hard.

Smoothie the Walrus didn't miss a beat. "In what way, a mistake? Is the charge against you a mistaken one, or—?"

"Not at all. The charge is quite true." (No point in her denying it: the evidence was overwhelming.) "I mean to say *I* was mistaken in my evaluation of a localized political situation. I was wrong about what was going on in Burma. And in Honduras as well—I was the one who drew Ambassador Aguirrez's attention to the rebel activity in San Pedro. I was also mistaken in presuming to take unilateral action in an attempt to correct the Burmese situation."

Li Xijuan's red aura positively *throbbed*. *Lies,* signaled Shelby.

"Then you regret having taken such action?"

"Yes."

No.

The walrus declared a recess. "Are you sure?" he asked Shelby. "Are you absolutely sure?"

"Absolutely. There's no mistaking that red glow. Li Xijuan is lying in her teeth. She doesn't regret arming the Burmese rebels in the least."

Martel pulled at his mustache. "But she knows *we* know she's lying. She's aware of what you're here for."

"And evidently doesn't care. Li Xijuan's a cool one. Maybe she wants people to know she's lying."

"Why would she want that?"

Shelby lifted her shoulders *I-don't-know.*

"Well," sighed the walrus, "keep your button-finger in good condition. We're in for a long session."

Ten hours. And twelve the next day. Twelve the day after that. Saturday and Sunday sessions. Li Xijuan's answers plotted a labyrinthine course of truth and falsehood and evasion and dissembling that succeeded in thoroughly confusing everybody. The unofficial records-keepers were reduced to color-coding her answers: this is a lie, this is not.

The commissioner from Israel, a gaunt woman in her fifties, was questioning Li Xijuan. "Did you deliberately seek out defective weapons to send to the Burmese?"

"I did."

"To sabotage their efforts?"

"Yes."

"Ambassador Aguirrez has testified that he tried to help the Militia by making sure its enemies would not succeed in any uprising they might attempt. Was that your purpose as well?"

"It was."

NoNoNoNoNo, Shelby signaled.

The Israeli woman paused. "Did you have any *additional* purpose for arming the Burmese?"

"None. My only purpose was to mitigate the dangers facing the Militia."

NO!

Eventually every member of the commission had a crack at shaking Li Xijuan's story. She didn't budge. Even when the commissioner from Brazil came right out and accused her of lying, Li Xijuan didn't so much as change expression.

"I am not lying," she lied.

"We have reason to think you are, Ambassador."

Li Xijuan didn't even glance in Shelby's direction. "You are mistaken."

And another time: "Did you propose this faulty-weapon plan to Ambassador Aguirrez?"

"I did."

"And to anyone else?"

"Yes." Volunteering nothing.

"To whom, Ambassador?"

"To Heinrich Schlimmermann, Ambassador from West Germany." Not holding it back, either.

Truth, Shelby's machine told the others. Li Xijuan was responsible for involving the other two. It was her show from the beginning.

In the end it was the commissioners who broke, not the Ambassador from China. After six straight days of intense questioning, **P. J.**

Martel declared a two-week recess for "re-evaluation and planning." Vacation. Li Xijuan left the hearing chamber unruffled and in complete control of herself.

In fact, she almost smiled.

CHAPTER 27

MY HAND IS IN
MY HUSSYFSKAP

"My hand is in my hussyfskap,
Goodman, as ye may see;
An it shoud nae be barrd this hundred year,
It's no be barrd for me."*

—"Get Up and Bar the Door,"
Middle English ballad

"I'm husbandless," Shelby told her sister. "Eric is gone."

"Gone?" said a shocked Tee. "What do you mean, gone?"

"I mean gone as in gone for good. He left for San Diego a week before he was scheduled to go. He told me I could pack up and come with him *right now*—or not come at all."

"An ultimatum?"

"Mm. So I wished him luck and called him a taxi. It's finally the end of the line for us."

Tee's mouth worked open and shut, open and shut. No words.

Shelby took hold of her sister's forearms and gave them a little shake. "Hey, it's okay. This is a *good* thing."

Tee was silent a moment. "Shelby, nobody takes the breakup of a marriage that casually. You and Eric loved each other once."

"I'm a slow reactor. It'll hit me later."

* Household duties.

"Come stay with Max and me," Tee said impulsively. "I think I'd better be around when, ah, it hits you."

"Thanks, Tee, that's nice of you. But I'm all right. Really."

Tee got an unusual look in her eye.

An hour later Shelby found herself in the Bradley apartment, apologizing to Max. "Tee insisted. She insists so seldom that I have no defenses when she does."

"I'm glad she did," said Max. "She's absolutely right. I'm sorry about Eric, Shelby. You're welcome to stay here as long as you like."

And no red aura.

"I've got to pick up my car before the garage closes," Max went on. "Just make yourself at home. We'll talk later, if you like. I'll be back in time for dinner—ah. That reminds me. Tee's planning to have artichokes again tonight. Think you could find out what she does to them?"

"What's to do? You drop them in boiling water."

"Yeah, but you know what they taste like. Play detective."

Slowly silently Shelby Kent Supersleuth tippy-toes in on little cat feet to the Gustum Gustorum of one Martita Bradley sister friend anti-cook. Oh for Merlin's cloak of invisibility or even Mr. H. G. Wells's nawsty chemical solution. There there she stands, the Morgana of meatloaf, scourge of the scallions, killer of artichokes. Yes trim the precious prickly little darlings carefully so carefully that's right Julia Child would love you. My sister the iron-and-vitamin supplemented huswyf reinforcing a cherished all-American-and-thensome ideal in her backlighted conservative-chic kitchen a living-color commercial for . . .

"Dammit," said Tee, sucking a bleeding finger.

. . . floor wax and anti-bad-odor sprays and stainless sinks and stickless skillets and you've-got-to-be-kidding foods. It's a plot a plot by UN enemies (Martians perhaps) the entire North American continent to sink slowly into the sea under the insupportable weight of mountains and mountains of Hamburger Helper. Good soldier Tee following General Commerce's orders guarding her typical kitchen post womanning her typical kitchen weapons . . .

. . . with a wholly untypical blue aura around her.

"Tee!" Shelby said sharply.

"What?" Tee jumped.

"Did you just say something out loud?"

"Christ, Shelby, don't do that. Not when I have a lethal weapon in my hand." She held up her paring knife, on which an artichoke was impaled.

"Sorry. Listen, Tee, answer me. Did you just say something?"

"No." Tee glanced around the kitchen. "Who would I be talking to?"

"Whom. Maybe you talk to yourself?"

"Never. Shel, what is this?"

"You were glowing blue just now."

Tee put down the stabbed artichoke. "Blue. *Blue?* But you've never . . ."

"No, I've never."

Intake of breath: "So you *can* read thoughts now!"

"No!" cried Shelby, frustrated. "I don't know what I was reading! I don't know what you were thinking, and I didn't hear you say anything. Except *dammit,* when you cut yourself. So why did you have a blue aura?"

"I think we'd better get some help," said Tee.

CHAPTER 28

DR. WIZARD OR DR. CALIGARI?

"Is anybody glowing now?" asked Dr. Wedner.

"No." Tee, Max, and Dr. Wedner were all aura-less.

"Has your sister glowed since the time you saw her in the kitchen?"

"No."

"And you're sure it was blue? Not some bluish shade of red, a purple?"

"It was about the color of that shirt you're wearing."

Dr. Wedner glanced down. "Light blue. Well then, Shelby, one isolated incident—"

"Is still an incident. I'm quoting you."

"I meant it wasn't much to go on. But you were right to call me." Dr. Wedner had hopped in his car and driven up from New Brunswick the minute Shelby phoned and told him what had happened.

"You don't seem very surprised," Max said.

"We were halfway expecting something like this. Ever since the tests showed Shelby's lie-detecting ability had achieved one hundred per cent accuracy."

"But what's more than one hundred per cent?" Max asked.

"That's what we have to find out," said Dr. Wedner. "You say you couldn't read your sister's mind when you saw her aura, Shelby?"

"No. Why is that the first thing everybody thinks of?"

"It's what we're most afraid of, I suppose. Mrs. Bradley," he said, turning to Tee, "I'm afraid I'm going to have to ask you to bare your culinary secrets. Will you tell us what you think about while you're trimming artichokes?"

"Well," Tee said hesitantly, "I was wondering whether Shelby really does like my cooking or whether she's just being polite."

A silence while everyone digested that. Then Shelby spoke: "I'm beginning to send as well as receive?"

"I knew it!" cried Tee. "You don't. Like my cooking."

"Let's try an experiment," said Dr. Wedner. "Mrs. Bradley, I want you to 'wonder' about something else, something you're not sure is true. Concentrate on it. Watch her carefully, Shelby."

They were quiet a moment. "Nothing," Shelby said.

"What were you thinking of, Mrs. Bradley?"

"I was wondering whether *Max* likes my cooking."

Max smiled blandly.

"Perhaps," said Dr. Wedner, "whatever this is works only in connection with your sister. Try it again, Mrs. Bradley, but this time think about Shelby."

Again, nothing.

"Well, Shelby," said Dr. Wedner, "I'm afraid this means more tests. You have two weeks off from the inquiry, don't you? Could you drive down tomorrow morning?"

"Yes, certainly."

"And Mrs. Bradley, you could help us enormously if you would come too."

"Me?" Tee was surprised.

"Yes, since it was your aura Shelby saw. Also, we'd like to give you a complete physical checkup."

"Why?"

"Many 'sensitives' are able to detect illness in their subjects by reading their auras correctly. It may be that your sister is developing that ability next. A physical exam would help confirm or eliminate that possibility. Will you come?"

"Uh, well, sure," said Tee, slightly shaken.

"What," asked Shelby, "did you think about? The last time?"

Tee didn't want to say, but Shelby pressed her. "I was wondering," Tee said reluctantly, "whether you'd be happier without Eric than you were with him."

"What's this?" Dr. Wedner said sharply. "What do you mean, happier without Eric?"

"My husband," Shelby announced dramatically, "has walked out on me."

"Eric left?"

"Today, as a matter of fact."

"Oh, I'm sorry." Dr. Wedner's face took on a pinched look. "I'm truly sorry, Shelby."

"No need to be," she said. "It's a relief, in a way."

"Still, it's a terrible thing to—"

"Hey, nobody died," Shelby smiled. "It's all right. Don't worry."

Dr. Wedner gave her a brave-little-woman look which was resented by—of all people—Tee.

"What she says is quite true," Tee snapped. "Here I am all prepared to be a tower-of-strength-in-her-time-of-need and she hasn't leaned once. Not once."

Properly chastised, Dr. Wedner smiled his goodbyes and left.

"Do you think," Max asked, "there could be some connection between Eric's leaving and this new aura? They both happened within a few hours of each other."

Shelby thought about it. "I don't see how."

"Nor I," echoed Tee.

"I don't either," Max admitted.

They left it at that.

CHAPTER 29

SACRE BLEU!

Tee looked around the laboratory with awe. "All this was built just to test my sister?"

"Not only built for her," said Dr. Wedner, "but designed for her as well. Most of it, anyway. We've never been able to 'measure' auras before your sister came along. She's unique."

"I'm a primitive," laughed Shelby.

Tee looked puzzled, so Dr. Wedner explained. "As a rule, sensitives who can read auras see many colors emanating from their subjects' bodies. Sometimes one color is dominant, but it melts into another color, which in turn melts into another, and so on through all the colors of the spectrum. Like layers of color surrounding the body. But Shelby sees only one color, red—in varying shades, but still the same basic color. And now she has seen blue—only once, so far, but again unaccompanied by any other color. Red and blue are both primary colors—that's why Shelby said she was a primitive. So if her ability to read blue develops fully, it's probable that she'll eventually begin to see people glowing yellow—the third of the primary colors."

"Ah. Wow."

"Wow indeed. Your sister's unique in another way. All the other sensitives we've tested have had to go into at least a light trance in order to see the auras at all. Shelby's able to perform her specialty in aura reading while remaining fully alert. That makes testing much easier. Speaking of tests, it's time for your physical, Mrs. Bradley."

Blood pressure a little low, but otherwise Tee was in good condition. Then the real testing began.

"The trouble is," Dr. Wedner said, "we don't really know what we're looking for. A specific thought, or pattern of thought? An emotional state? Melancholy's the first thing that comes to mind—that 'blue' state we all get into every once in a while. We'll just have to try everything we can think of."

Old hand Shelby took it all in stride, but after four days the testing procedures were beginning to get Tee down.

"I hate it," she confided to her sister. "I don't see how you do it, Shelby! They just . . . keep at us, all the time. I don't like having my head wired up every day, I miss Max, I miss my piano, and—"

"And you're doing it again."

"Doing what?"

"Glowing blue."

Small voice: "I am?"

"Dr. Wedner! *Dr. Wedner!*"

He came running. "Now?"

"Now."

Tee was whisked away. After examining her, Dr. Wedner's staff put forth the theory that the cause of the blue aura was nothing more than simple anxiety.

"Right," grinned Dr. Wedner. "Incredible the way the mind intuits the truth long before even a shred of scientific evidence appears to back it up. Singin' the blues, I get the blues when it rains—almost a joke, isn't it? But right on target. Mrs. Bradley—"

"Tee, please."

"All right—Tee. Tee was wondering about your opinion of her cooking, Shelby, when you first saw the blue aura. That was on a conscious level. But she'd just learned a few hours earlier that your marriage had broken up. That upset her, naturally. So her anxiety about you lingered on on an unconscious level even while she was thinking of artichokes or whatever. It was so obvious an explanation that I tended to distrust it."

"So there *was* a connection between Eric's leaving and the blue aura," Tee said.

"Definitely. The ability to read suppressed worry, anxiety—it's been latent in Shelby since birth, developing at its own speed. Eric's departure was the strong trigger needed to bring it out. The sympathy between you two was right, and Shelby was able to—"

"That man over there is blue," Shelby interrupted.

"Great!" yelled Dr. Wedner. "Now we're moving—it's broken through. Wait fifteen minutes while I set something up."

Twenty minutes later: Shelby, Dr. Wedner, and Tee sitting in a small room, looking through one-way glass into an even smaller room. Just like a police station.

"I've lined up some of the technicians for you to look at, Shelby. They'll come in one at a time. Examine them carefully, and tell me what you see." Dr. Wedner signaled for the first technician to enter.

"Robin's-egg blue," Shelby said promptly.

"Good," Dr. Wedner nodded. "That's Johnson. He's a chronic worrier. If anyone's likely to give off a blue aura, he's the one." He pushed a button that lit a light that told the man named Johnson he could leave.

The next four, nothing.

Shelby whistled when the next technician entered, a woman in her late twenties. "Royal blue."

"Hm," said Dr. Wedner. "I've heard she—well, we'll check them all out. Now for the last one."

Shelby blanched.

Wedner, quick to notice: "What is it?"

"Navy blue, almost black. That man's in trouble."

Dr. Wedner gave her a sharp look. "All right. We'll take care of it. If he is in trouble, we'll see he gets the help he needs."

The two weeks finally ended.

"It's a strange gift, Shelby," Dr. Wedner said, "and a godsend. If this develops the way I think it will, you may well reach the point where you can diagnose anxiety-based mental illness with the same degree of accuracy you can now detect lies."

"I'm feeling a little blue myself," Shelby sighed. "Tell me something about all the good I'll be doing mankind."

Dr. Wedner laughed. "Personally, I'm looking forward to that yellow aura. I'm positive it won't end here."

"Can we go home now?" asked Tee.

CHAPTER 30

PETER QUINCE
OR PETER QUINT?

"Ambassador Schlimmermann," said Martel the walrus, "are *you* going to tell us that aiding dissidents helps preserve the Militia?"

"Precisely," said Schlimmermann precisely.

"By providing them with live explosives? Your two confederates supplied their rebels with *faulty* weapons, but you—"

"That is their concern. I am not responsible for their misconceptions. Allow me to explain. It's clear that none of you understand how established authority retains its authority."

"Enlighten us," sniffed the walrus.

Schlimmermann cleared his throat. "Any unchallenged authority stagnates. Automatically. When there's no outside threat to its solidarity, it grows complacent, smug. And sloppy. Efficiency decreases—"

"Just a minute," Martel interrupted. "Are you saying that a peaceful government *must* be an inefficient one?"

"Of course." Schlimmermann lifted an eyebrow. "Once an institution has achieved absolute power, it dies of overweight. Like the Roman Empire. Totally decadent! Rome could no longer defend itself. And why? Internal decay."

And malaria, thought Shelby. *And famine. And the division of military forces between Rome and Byzantium. And a few other minor contributory factors like that.*

"So if the Militia is to succeed," Schlimmermann continued, "it must not be allowed to grow fat. It must be challenged—immediately, constantly. Aggression is as natural to the human animal as breathing. By providing small, *containable* rebellions, we prevent the larger collapse that would otherwise be inevitable."

Every one of the commissioners was sitting open-mouthed. Before Shelby could stop herself, she laughed out loud. *Pop Philosophy 101. Three credits.*

One of the commissioners roused himself enough to signal Shelby. *Yes,* she signaled back. The damned fool wasn't lying. He really did believe the world could be protected against its own violent tendencies through a simple process of inoculation. As if the world had never been exposed to that particular disease before.

"Ambassador Schlimmermann," said the walrus with barely suppressed anger, "I think that's a load of crap." (*Good for double-you.*) "But even if it were true, why manufacture rebellions? Everyone will not be satisfied with an international militia. Opposition is bound to develop on its own—"

"Too unreliable." Schlimmermann dismissed Martel's objection with a wave of his hand. "We've never had an international militia before, but that doesn't mean we can't anticipate its problems. Please try to understand. Every form of opposition from satire to nuclear warfare carries a kind of compliment in it. It says to its target: 'We recognize you have a style, an importance . . . a *something* we're afraid of. Otherwise we wouldn't bother to attack.'"

You always love the one you hurt?

"But—"

"Allow me to finish, please. Attacking a sacred office—and I firmly believe the mission of the Militia to be a sacred one—attacking a sacred office, I say, is a way of reinforcing it. To defy the Militia is to acknowledge its power and accept its authority. Surely you see the logic of that? Attacks on the Establishment are necessary to the preservation of the Establishment. And surely you must agree that enforcing the Militia's authority is far too important to leave to chance. Rebellions must be timed carefully, and they must be controlled."

A ten-second pause—then the entire hearing chamber started talking. Among the mutterings here and there Shelby detected snatches of hysterical laughter. *This isn't happening,* she thought. *They're acting as if this were a legitimate proposition worth refuting. All those people dead—because of this arrogant schlemiel and his two fellow puppet masters. Send them to the funny farm and have done with it.*

"Disgusting!"

"Sick, sick, sick!"

Go ahead—yell, if it makes you feel better. Shelby felt herself growing light-headed from all the absurdity around her. *You're just proving his point—by attacking him, you make him important.* Schlimmermann: a rock island of calm in the hurricane. *Puff yourself up, little man; you'll never know another moment like this one.*

"The time has come," thundered the walrus, "for us to get a few things straight!"

The time has come, the walrus said, to ask a few of those overwhelming questions Saint Thomas à Eliot was so fond of dropping into people's dinner plates. Such as: Are there caribou in Malibu?

"How," continued the thunder, "did you ever expect to get away with it?"

"I didn't."

Is Plato's cave in Disneyland?

"Then why do it, if you knew you'd be stopped?"

"I am convinced my actions will serve to make the Security Council aware of the danger, perhaps even to inspire others to take up where I left off."

Was Lamont Cranston overshadowed by Larry Talbot?

"Over five thousand people are dead because of what you and Li Xijuan and Mañuel Aguirrez have done. You call this a *contained* rebellion?"

"Yes. It went no further than I'd anticipated."

Did Sherlock Holmes and Dr. Watson have a homosexual relationship?

"Do you—?"

"Stop it!" Shelby was on her feet, pulling off her earphone. "Don't dignify this egomaniac by taking him seriously."

And to everyone's astonishment, she walked out.

CHAPTER 31

I'M SORRY

"I'm sorry," wailed Tee. "I don't do it on purpose!"

"I know you don't, Tee. But that's an awfully bright blue you're sending out."

"Maybe sunglasses . . . ?"

"No, no."

"And I wanted you to be able to come here and relax! Look." Tee gestured toward the dining table, which was literally covered with food. A bottle of wine. Kreplach soup, coleslaw, cheese, rice crackers, chicken salad, cold roast beef, corn rye bread, and two huge sour pickles. "I ordered it all from the delicatessen. *I didn't cook a thing.*"

"Oh, Tee." Shelby laughed, and hugged her sister. "Where's Max?"

"In Philadelphia. On an emergency call."

"An emergency scene design call?"

"Some show that's in trouble. Out-of-town tryouts. The producer decided the look of the show was all wrong, so he asked Max to come see what he could do. Max says the first-act set is made up solely of tiers of bleachers holding lawn mowers. Two hundred lawn mowers."

"Oh, dear!"

"Yeah, one of *those.*" *Squeak, squeak.* Tee was working her hand exercisers all the time she was talking; one of the grips needed oiling. "Was it awful today, Shelby?" *Squeak, squeak, squeak.*

Shelby shrugged. "Another day, another fifty cents."

"It looked awful on TV." *Squeak, squeak.* "I would never have had the courage to walk out."

"Do you think I was wrong to leave?"

Squeaksqueaksqueaksqueaksqueak. "It's hard to say, Shel. It was all so confused."

"That's why I walked—it was getting out of hand. Put that thing down, Tee, it's driving me nuts. Schlimmermann was getting all . . ." Her voice trailed off as the phone rang.

It was Eric, calling from San Diego. "Shelby? I thought you'd be at Tee's. I wanted to tell you you were magnificent! Simply magnificent! I was watching every minute of it, and I'm proud of you."

"I'm glad you're pleased."

"When you got up and walked out on them, I stood up and cheered! Actually cheered! This means you're through with the inquiry, aren't you?"

"No, I'm not."

"What? What did you say?"

"I said I'm going back tomorrow."

He hung up on her.

Prick.

"Have we lost our lie detector?" P. J. Martel asked.

"No, I don't think so—I've sent Gilbert to talk to her. I'm sorry she stalked out like that." Sir John Dudley lowered himself into "his" chair in Martel's office. "Good news—we've got what you want. Evidence that Schlimmermann arranged for the bombings in Greece."

"Hah!" A big smile.

"He went through a very intricate chain of command, but we needed only one link to get the rest of the chain. And we've got him —the man who gave the order to the man who gave the order to the man who bought the explosives. And he's talking."

"Excellent. I can't tell you how relieved I am, Sir John," Martel said. "Schlimmermann has shown no indication of denying his responsibility for Greece, but I for one could never vote to indict without external confirming evidence. Any nut could walk in and claim he did it. And Schlimmermann *is* something of a nut."

Sir John grunted. "You have to be mad to kill three thousand people just to prove a point. If he is indicted, he'll probably plead insanity."

"And probably get away with it," Martel scowled.

Shelby got back to her apartment building to find Kevin Gilbert waiting out front in a car. She opened the car door and got in; it was too cold to stand outside and talk and she was too tired to invite him in. "Yes, I'll be there tomorrow morning," she answered before he could ask.

He smiled. "Well, that takes care of that. You look beat."

"It's been a busy day. Am I in trouble with your boss?"

"No, Sir John didn't bat an eye. Martel might not be too happy at your upstaging him, though."

Shelby sighed. "I shouldn't have let Schlimmermann get to me the way he did. That arrogant . . . the man belongs in a cage."

"He'll be in one soon." Kevin hesitated. "Shelby, this is the first time we've had a chance to talk since before the two-week recess. I'm sorry about your marriage—breakups are never easy. I'm sorry."

She slid her eyes away from the reddish glow around his body.

He noticed. "All right, I'm not sorry. Shelby, do you remember the first time we talked? In that bar on Lexington Avenue? You spoke of your sister with love and concern. But you mentioned your husband only offhandedly, as the focal point of a problem you had to deal with. So no, I'm not sorry. I'm sorry you have to go through the unpleasantness of a breakup, but I can't work up any real anxieties over the fact that Eric Kent is out of your life. He *is* out, isn't he? Permanently?"

"Without a doubt," said Shelby, remembering the phone conversation earlier in the evening.

"In that case," said Kevin, "what are you doing tomorrow night?"

CHAPTER 32

PRINCE ALBERT IN A CAN

BARBARA: Killing. Is that your remedy for everything?
UNDERSHAFT: It is the final test of conviction, the only
lever strong enough to overturn a social system, the only
way of saying Must. . . . Your pious mob fills up ballot
papers and imagines it is governing its masters; but the
ballot paper that really governs is the paper that has a bul-
let wrapped up in it.

—G. B. Shaw, *Major Barbara*

"Well, Mrs. Kent?" growled the walrus. "Will you be staying the entire session today?"

Shelby smiled sheepishly. "I'm sorry about yesterday. It won't
happen again, I give you my word."

They were in a small room down the hall from the hearing chamber, gearing up for another go at Schlimmermann. "Unofficially, I
don't really blame you," sighed Martel. "I'm sometimes tempted to
head out to the Kuala Lumpur Hilton myself."

Shelby accepted the tactful reminder that none of them liked what
was going on. "What happens now?"

"Now we try to find out why the explosives Schlimmermann had
shipped to Greece were *not* defective. The generals must have disagreed about how to run their private war. We've got to get that
cleared up before we vote on an indictment. Some members of the
commission want to include a recommendation if we do indict—a rec-

ommendation either to execute or to toss the three of them into a loony bin."

"They belong in a loony bin."

"But that has its drawbacks," Martel mused, more to himself than to Shelby. "Do we make Ezra Pounds out of them? Aguirrez's martyr complex is already getting a big workout. And Schlimmermann— well, you pegged him right. An egomaniac. I'm beginning to suspect we'll never know what's going on in Li Xijuan's mind."

"Won't executing them make them even bigger martyrs?"

"For a while. But people have short memories. As long as these three are in confinement, they'll be a constant reminder of their 'self-sacrifice,' as they see it. Have you read the newspapers this morning? Already our conspirators are beginning to acquire heroic status."

"*Heroic!?!*"

The old man snorted. "How many people do you think really understood all that rigamarole of Schlimmermann's? To most of the television viewers he came off as a militant nonconformist, advocating open rebellion against the Establishment. Everybody's favorite target."

"But that's just the opposite of what he said!"

"I know it, and you know it, but the people—that great, seething mass we're here to serve—the *people* simply don't listen very carefully. Half of them hate Schlimmermann because he's a 'rebel,' and half of them love him for the same reason. And Schlimmermann's no rebel—he's a rigid authoritarian who'll kill indiscriminately to maintain not his own authority, which would at least be understandable, but the idea of authority."

"In other words, a nut."

"That's where the trouble comes in. Men have been willing to kill for ideas before. Do we judge Schlimmermann insane because his idea is such a repugnant one?"

"Yes."

The walrus looked startled, and then laughed. "You sound very positive."

"I'm not, really." A moment passed. Then Shelby said, "I think I ought to tell you I'm beginning to develop the ability to read a new aura—one that reveals anxiety and depression."

Martel's eyebrows shot up. "A new aura? Will it interfere with—?"

"No, not at all. There's no confusion between the two. The new one is a different color entirely. For instance, you've been glowing light blue during this entire conversation. All that means is that you're worried—hardly surprising, considering the line of work you're in. But by the time this new power is fully developed, I may be able to diagnose cases of extreme anxiety that result in mental illness. But I'm not to that point yet."

"How long until you are? In time to help us decide about Schlimmermann and the other two?"

Shelby shook her head. "My lie-detecting ability took fourteen years to reach its peak. I was a child when I first saw an aura—in the form of a faint pink ring around my father's body. But it wasn't until a few years ago that it became totally reliable. But Dr. Wedner says it will probably go faster this time—"

"Wedner? Oh yes, the Rutgers man, right. Go on."

"He says the fact that I started off seeing different shades of blue indicates a shorter development time. But don't count on anything—the testing procedures alone take more time than this inquiry will be in session. Right now all the blue aura tells me is when people are worried or upset. Even when they hide it as well as you do."

A walrus-smile. "My dear, I hope I'm still around when you can 'read' mental illness. You'll solve a lot of problems for us."

"Or create them," Shelby said glumly.

He laughed. "I'll bet you're giving off a blue aura yourself." He glanced at his watch. "Time for the circus to begin. Let's go hear what our murderous peer has to tell us today."

CHAPTER 33

SPRINGES TO CATCH WOODCOCKS

P. J. Martel sat silent, immobile, his eyes closed. Content to let the Indian member of the commission carry the ball for a while.

"Ambassador Schlimmermann," said the Indian, "do you deny arranging the purchase of two hundred pounds of gelignite through a Zürich distributor named Franz Meier?"

"One moment please." Schlimmermann leaned forward in his chair. "Before I answer any more questions, I have a demand to make of this commission. I want that woman removed from this hearing chamber." And he pointed at Shelby.

"Who, me?" Shelby whispered to the lawyer sitting next to her.

Martel opened one eye at the word "demand" but said nothing.

"Mrs. Kent is part of our staff," the Indian said. "She has every legal right to be here."

"She has no legal right to call me an egomaniac," Schlimmermann barked. "I want her out of here."

The Indian looked toward Martel. The walrus stirred. "Herr Schlimmermann. May I remind you that you are not the one to lay down the conditions of this inquiry? Mrs. Kent stays. But you are quite correct in one thing—she had no right to call you an egomaniac. I think an apology is in order. Before you object"—cutting off the German before he could say anything—"perhaps I should remind you this inquiry is providing you with the only public forum you will have. If you wish to explain your position *publicly,* I suggest you accept Mrs. Kent's apology."

Schlimmermann glared at Martel a moment and then said, "I haven't heard any apology yet."

The walrus leaned back in his chair, looked over his shoulder at Shelby, and cocked a bushy eyebrow at her.

"Uh, yes, well," Shelby stammered. "I apologize for calling you an egomaniac, Ambassador."

"There you are," said the walrus, and went back into his coma.

Schlimmermann didn't deign to answer either of them. Shelby noticed Li Xijuan watching the exchange with amusement in her eyes. Aguirrez, slumped in his chair, glowing blue, hadn't heard a word that was said.

The Indian started to repeat his question about the gelignite but Schlimmermann interrupted him impatiently. "Yes, yes, I ordered it. Why keep going on about it? I arranged the bombing of the Militia Supply Headquarters in Athens and the garrison near the Albanian border."

"As part of the, ah, *contained* rebellion you were telling us about."

"Precisely. There has long been much unco-ordinated guerrilla activity in Greece. I provided the rebels with a focus for their hostility. With no further explosives or arms available to them, they will live on the so-called glory of their two-pronged attack on the Militia for years to come. They are temporarily purged. Greece will be quiescent now—for as long, it is to be hoped, as it takes the Militia to establish its authority beyond challenge."

"No guerrillas died in those attacks that we know of. All the casualties were Militiamen and UN employees, and some passersby."

"I believe that is correct."

"A strange way to 'help' the Militia."

A shrug. "Your opinion."

"Over thirty-two hundred people died in Greece. *Thirty-two hundred*. Do you fully understand, Herr Schlimmermann, that you caused the deaths of thirty-two hundred innocent people?"

Schlimmermann looked the Indian straight in the eye. "I understand perfectly."

"And it means nothing to you?"

The German's mouth twitched. "I'd say it means more to me than it does to you. I see it as an accurate gauge of the extent of the difficulties facing us—by us, I mean the UN. In an efficiently run society such extreme corrective measures would not be necessary. You want me to say I'm sorry? Very well, I'm sorry their deaths were necessary. But they *were* necessary."

"Would you do the same thing again?"

"Without a moment's hesitation."

The Indian's voice softened. "Ambassador, your cavalier attitude toward human life is totally beyond my comprehension. You come before the eyes of the world and admit to being a mass murderer—and in the service of what? *Efficiency?*"

"Mass murderer?" Schlimmermann didn't laugh, but he looked as if he wanted to. "Yes, you need these little labels, don't you? To sanction your own feeling of righteousness. I prefer to think of myself as a physician, practicing preventive medicine."

"Arrogant goddamned egomaniac," Shelby muttered under her breath.

"Hush," whispered the lawyer next to her.

The Indian decided on a new tack. "Ambassador Aguirrez has testified that the plan was to supply insurgents with defective weapons, to avoid endangering the lives of the UN peacekeeping forces involved in the action. Yet you supplied the Greek guerrillas with live explosives. Can you explain that?"

Schlimmermann shrugged. "This business of supplying defective weapons—that's only playing at rebellion. In order for the plan to work, the threat to the world's security had to be a real one. Old grenades with faulty firing pins just wouldn't do the job. Providing that kind of weapon is too tentative, too half-hearted. Even cowardly."

"So you disagreed with Ambassador Aguirrez and Ambassador Li as to the best way of staging contained rebellions."

"I disagreed from the start. I agreed to the idea of controlling rebellions, but I disagreed as to the most effective method of doing so."

Schlimmermann talked on, expounding on his theory for maintaining authority by manipulating those who would rebel against it. Occasionally a light on Shelby's machine would flash on. *Yes,* she'd signal; the Ambassador from West Germany wasn't lying about his motives. Out of the corner of her eye she caught a movement and unconsciously turned her head to see what caused it. What she saw made her gasp.

Aguirrez—surrounded by a depression-aura that *moved.* Not the mild pulsations of the red aura of deceit, but blue-black waves rushing away from his body, faster and faster and darker and darker.

Shelby jumped up from her chair and ran to the walrus's side. "Aguirrez has gone into a deep depression," she said in a low voice. "I think he's suicidal—he might do something desperate unless he gets help *right now*."

Martel didn't have to be told twice. He muttered instructions to one of his aides. Almost immediately two security guards hurried to Aguirrez and led him gently but firmly from the hearing chamber. The Mexican moved like a sleepwalker—sluggish, oblivious to everything around him. Martel declared a recess.

"Tell me what it looked like," he commanded.

Shelby described the aura the best she could. "I've never seen anything like it," she concluded, shaken.

The walrus looked at her in sudden sympathy. "This isn't going to be easy for you, is it? This new aura. Has it appeared around Schlimmermann?"

"No." All around her, people were gathering up papers, speculating quietly over Aguirrez's unexpected departure, departing themselves. Shelby started to leave too when she felt eyes burning into the back of her head. She turned to find Heinrich Schlimmermann staring at her.

With undisguised hatred.

She'd jumped up and run to the walrus in her concern for Aguirrez, ignoring everything else that was going on in the hearing chamber. She'd caused Martel to take action that disrupted the inquiry, cutting off the German's metaphysical musings in midsentence. Of course Schlimmermann hated her.

She'd killed his act.

CHAPTER 34

WARNER OLAND
OR SIDNEY TOLER?

FRANCISCO: All my plots
Turn back upon myself; but I am in,
And must go on . . .
One deadly sin, then, help to cure
another.

—Philip Massinger, *The Duke of Milan*

"Catatonic," Sir John Dudley said. "The man's withdrawn completely."

P. J. Martel blew out air through his thick lips. "Responsibility too much for him. So he just resigned." Mañuel Aguirrez was in a private clinic in upstate New York—isolated, incommunicado, *gone.* "He saw the deaths of the Honduran rebels as beneficent—they were the bad guys, no two ways about it, period. But Schlimmermann's slaughter of three thousand innocent people—that must have brought home to Aguirrez exactly what he was involved in. Even though Aguirrez was a mass murderer himself, he still had more conscience than his two co-conspirators put together. A believer in instant solutions, Señor Aguirrez! Foolish, foolish man. What do the doctors say?"

"As little as possible. They certainly hold out no hope for a recovery."

"Well, that settles one-third of our problem. We can't vote to indict a catatonic—which means the inquiry will have to be open-ended, in case Aguirrez does manage to pull out of it. The doctors didn't rule out the possibility altogether, did they?"

"They just don't know," Sir John said. "There's no way of telling. But the message they were sending was don't count on it."

Martel wagged his big head back and forth. "You reach a point in your life when you think you can't be shocked any further. Nothing human beings do surprises you any longer. But their motives! Their motives get you every time."

The two old men sat quietly a moment, musing. Then Martel continued, "I still don't know why any of this happened. Aguirrez says he wanted to sabotage insurgents to protect the Militia. Schlimmermann says he wanted to aid the insurgents as a way of dramatizing the Militia's authority. Li Xijuan says she agrees with Aguirrez, but Shelby Kent says she's lying. Does that mean Li Xijuan agrees with Schlimmermann after all? Then why send *defective* weapons to the Burmese? I think we're going to have to recall Ambassador Li."

Sir John nodded. "For the record."

Martel glanced at him sharply. "Meaning we won't learn anything new? Possibly. But I'm interested in finding out how Li Xijuan happened to settle on those two—Aguirrez thinking social ills can be cured with force and Schlimmermann ego-tripping on some private power game in which he's the only player. Strange choices."

"But they did the job, didn't they?"

"I'm still not sure what the job was. Protecting the Militia? Attacking it?"

"Ambassador," said Sir John, "have you considered the possibility that these attacks on the Militia were not the ultimate end of Li Xijuan's scheming? That they were, perhaps, the means to a different end?"

Martel looked dubious. "What end?"

"I don't know. But she doesn't seem overly concerned whether the attacks succeeded or not. Only that they took place. She may have selected Aguirrez and Schlimmermann as her confederates solely because they were willing to co-operate—the fact that the two men disagreed on method may not have been important. We don't know these two were the only delegates she approached."

"Oh, surely not! Any ambassador who had a clue of what she was intending would have spoken up about it."

"Would he have?" Sir John said quietly.

Martel's face changed. "Guilt by association, you mean?"

"Mmm. Say Ambassador Li approaches Ambassador X and drops a hint or two about 'helping' the Militia in certain unorthodox ways. What if word of that got back to Ambassador X's superiors? Might they not begin to wonder what there was in Ambassador X to make Li Xijuan think he might be willing to co-operate in such a venture? Would Ambassador X speak up and denounce Ambassador Li?"

"Depends on who Ambassador X is," Martel said heavily. "Some of them probably would want to keep it quiet."

"Especially when they're not quite sure what Li Xijuan was getting at. Her approach would have been oblique, enigmatic. Vague enough that she could deny everything if someone were foolhardy enough to speak up. Oh, she would manage that all right. Li Xijuan is an even more skillful manipulator of people than Schlimmermann. No, Ambassador X wouldn't know what to do. So he'd end up just keeping his mouth shut."

"But *why?*" Martel slapped the top of his desk in frustration and then looked surprised at himself. "What does she want?"

"I can't say what she wants, but I do know what she's got. Something the rest of us have all been looking on as merely an annoying by-product of this inquiry."

"And that is?"

"Publicity."

Martel's shaggy eyebrows rose. "She's done all this for publicity?"

"A possibility," Sir John cautioned.

"Personal publicity? I can't believe that."

"Not personal publicity. Li Xijuan is not the ego-driven creature Schlimmermann is. If she *is* trying to draw attention to something, we don't know what it is yet."

Martel's big head seemed to sink lower into his shoulders. "Good God in heaven. What are we involved in?"

Sir John didn't answer. He wasn't ready to tell Martel about an investigation he'd just put in motion—nothing might come of it, after all; it was what the Americans called a long shot. Li Xijuan had given most of her adult life to the UN, working her way up from a minor assistant in the Chinese delegation to Ambassador, surviving the changes in the political winds blowing through her homeland. She had made her mark on history with her work in establishing the Militia. But Sir John suspected it wasn't the UN that held the answer they were all looking for.

He thought the answer lay in China.

CHAPTER 35

HURRY UP PLEASE IT'S TIME

Music is a habit, like spitting.

—Percy Grainger, as quoted on the
BBC program(me?) *My Music*

"Meet Kevin Gilbert," Shelby said. "Kevin, this is my sister, Tee. My brother-in-law, Max."

"Pleased to meet you," said Tee, and burst into tears.

"What? What?" said Shelby.

"Max says," Tee snurfled, "Max says he's going to string me up by my thumbs!"

"Neater than boiling in oil," Max said cheerily and stuck out a hand. "Kevin? You're just in time for round four."

"Ah, mumph, yuh," said Kevin, shaking hands.

"But what's it all about?" Shelby demanded.

"Max has turned into a monster," Tee said. "That's all. A monster."

"No more Mr. Nice Guy." Max gave a stage-villain snarl. "Things is a-gunna change round he-ah."

Kevin: "Uh, maybe we should come back later."

"Nonsense, we need an audience. I'm going to fix us drinks, and we can all have a nice drunken brawl." Max squinted an eye at Kevin. "Scotch." It wasn't a question.

Kevin grinned. "Have you thought of going into intelligence work?"

Shelby: *"What is going on?"*

"Wait until that *monster* leaves," Tee said, "and I'll tell you." The monster obligingly went into the kitchen to fix the drinks. "Shelby, remember the Three Rivers Piano Competition?"

"Of course I do."

"Well, one of the judges is now the assistant conductor of the Boston Symphony. He's scheduled to conduct the Prokofieff and his soloist canceled out on him and he remembered I played it in the Competition and—"

"And he wants you to step in!" Shelby shouted. "Fantastic!"

"And my monster husband is threatening all sorts of dire things if I don't—"

"And he should, he should! My God, Tee, what an opportunity! The Boston Symphony!"

"Yeah," Tee shivered. "The Boston Symphony."

"Congratulations?" Kevin ventured, not sure this was what was called for.

"Uh-huh, thanks, I don't know—"

"Now, Tee," said Shelby, her voice rising, *"you are not going to say no.* It's the chance of a lifetime!"

"Yep," said Max, coming back with the drinks. "Old Steel Fingers here has a chance to show her stuff. *And she's going to do it.*"

"Max, it's only two months from now," Tee protested. "I can't be ready in two months."

"You're ready *now,*" Max and Shelby said together.

"You're bullies," Tee accused. "Both of you. Bullies."

"I'm a monster," Max reminded her. "Shelby can be the bully."

Tee cast around for an adequate expression of her indignation at being bullied and came up with a cliché. "After giving you the best years of my life—"

"Oh tush, you haven't even reached your best years yet," Max said amiably. "Accept it, Tee. This time you're just not going to get away with copping out."

Feeling something like a fifth wheel, Kevin sank down into a leather armchair, winced, and pulled one of Tee's handgrips from under him.

"Now I want you to repeat after me," Max said. " 'I'm going to do it.' Come on now. 'I'm going to do it.' Say it."

Tee seemed to be having trouble breathing.

Max: " 'I'm going to do it.' You can say it."

Tee swallowed three times, fast.

"Say it, Tee," Shelby half commanded, half pleaded.

Max repeated it for her. " 'I'm going to do it.' "

Tee took a deep breath. "I'm."

"That's the first step!" Max exulted. "Come on, Tee. Say the rest of it."

"I'm going to."

"You're going to what?"

"I'm going to do it!"

Kevin Gilbert joined in the cheering that greeted this display of determination. What it had cost Tee to commit herself was something he'd never fully understand, but he could recognize a turning point when he saw one.

"See?" said Shelby. "Didn't hurt a bit, did it?"

"I'm going to do it," Tee repeated wonderingly.

"Of course you are. And you're going to do it *beautifully*." Shelby hugged her sister and blew a kiss to Max. "That's a great monster husband you've got there, kiddo."

Tee turned to Max and smiled. "I'm going to do it."

He enfolded her in a bear hug. "Just keep saying it."

"What's the matter?" Kevin asked Shelby.

"I want to cry," she said apologetically.

"Understandable."

"No, Tee's the one who blubbers. I'm the stalwart one."

"Oh, I didn't understand," he laughed and finished his drink. "Would I be overstepping my role as guest if I fixed us refills?"

Shelby looked over to where Tee and Max were wrapped up in each other. "I don't think anyone would even notice."

Kevin took her glass and went into the kitchen. Shelby felt suddenly drained—kitten-weak, in fact. And happy. Happier than she'd been in years. She watched the two people who were the most important in the world to her and she felt good.

"I'm going to do it," Tee beamed. "I really am."

CHAPTER 36

WOODCOCK TO MINE OWN SPRINGE

*So those who thirst for glory smother
Secret weakness and longing, neither
Weep nor sigh nor listen to the sickness
In their souls.*

—"The Wanderer," anonymous
eighth-century poem

P. J. Martel and Li Xijuan were eying each other carefully, cat and mouse. But it wasn't clear to Shelby which was the cat and which the mouse.

Martel started it off. "You say you provided faulty weapons to the insurgents for the purpose of protecting the Militia."

"That is correct."

"And you say that was your only purpose."

"That is also correct."

No, Shelby signaled once again.

"Ambassador Li, I suggest you are withholding something. You have some other purpose in mind that you are not telling us."

"What purpose could that be?"

"Suppose you tell us. We know you're motivated by something other than concern for the welfare of the Militia."

"The Militia has long been my primary concern."

"And thereby makes a perfect cover," the walrus said smoothly.

"But it's no good, Ambassador. We know you've been lying to us."

"You can prove this, of course?"

Martel grumbled something under his breath. She had him there; by now everyone knew Shelby's testimony was not admissible in any court of law. But the walrus didn't give up. "We don't have to prove it, Ambassador. This is an inquiry, not a trial. If we are convinced you are lying to us, then we must act in accordance with the dictates of our own judgment."

"Then I must rely upon your sense of fair play, mustn't I?" the Chinese woman said calmly.

The walrus let a silence develop. Then, rapidly: "Did you ask any delegates other than Ambassadors Aguirrez and Schlimmermann to join you in your plan to sabotage rebellions?"

"No, I did not."

Lie.

Martel flicked his eye at Shelby's machine and said, "We have information that says you did."

Li Xijuan gave her almost-smile. "Then produce it."

Shelby knew Martel well enough by now that she could see he was uncomfortable. He didn't like being cast in the role of bullying inquisitor, hinting at evidence but never producing it. It was a sure-fire way of generating sympathy for this murderess who sat before them.

He backed off. "What made you choose Ambassador Aguirrez and Ambassador Schlimmermann as your partners?"

"They are both men of action. They are not afraid to run personal risks in order to achieve a greater good."

Martel almost groaned; slogans again. "A greater good. Are you saying the only way to deal with malcontents is to kill them?"

"There are degrees of discontent. They can't all be treated the same."

"Ambassador Li, where did you get the idea that you had the right to pass judgment on those people? You are a member of a lawmaking body, but that does not make *you* the law."

"I have already said it was a mistake."

"And I don't believe you. I believe you look upon the law as merely a tool to be used for your own purposes."

"You are mistaken. It is only Herr Schlimmermann who assumes the laws of the universe are suspended just for him," Li Xijuan said in a voice so bland that it took everyone a moment to understand exactly what she'd said.

Schlimmermann glanced at the Chinese woman condescendingly and then looked away again. Not worth answering.

Thieves fall out? Martel wondered. More likely a diversionary tactic, but one worth following up. "We know Herr Schlimmermann disagreed with you and Señor Aguirrez as to tactics. Is that what you're referring to?"

"Yes," Li Xijuan said shortly.

"And perhaps motivation as well?"

"That too—they are interrelated, cause and effect. I wish to emphasize it was not my purpose to see that members of the Militia were harmed in any way. The deaths of the Militiamen stationed in Greece were the work of the Ambassador from West Germany, who acted more out of personal motives than from any sense of political responsibility."

Martel looked at Shelby's machine and almost gloated out loud when he saw Li Xijuan was not lying. She had told them something after all: her own motivation was different from Schlimmermann's. Whatever the reason was for what she'd done, it was political, *not* personal. As he'd suspected. Martel ignored the murmurings in the hearing chamber while he thought about it. Maybe he should take the bait Li Xijuan had dangled in front of him. The alternative was to keep pressing for the Chinese woman's true motive, a line of inquiry that had already proved a dead end more than once. He decided: Li Xijuan was dismissed and Heinrich Schlimmermann recalled.

A wild idea: "Are you a neo-Nazi, Herr Schlimmermann?"

Schlimmermann laughed out loud. "Certainly not. Please do not associate me with those bumblers."

"Neo-Nazis are bumblers?"

"I was referring to the original Nazi party. The neo-Nazis aren't even a party—just groups of ineffectual men living on dreams of lost glory." Contemptuously.

Truth, Shelby signaled.

"You called them bumblers," Martel said. "So you disapprove of the Nazis because they were failures?"

"Yes," said Schlimmermann.

Yes, echoed Shelby.

Martel dropped his voice to a near whisper. "But you have no moral objection to what they did?"

Even the sound of paper rustling stopped as everyone in the chamber waited for Schlimmermann's answer. The German ran his tongue over suddenly dry lips. "I do not approve of their persecution of the Jews," he said carefully.

Shelby signaled *Yes*.

"On moral grounds?" Martel persisted.

"On moral grounds, of course."

No.

"You're lying," Martel said bluntly.

Schlimmermann shot a look of disgust at Shelby and said, "It was the biggest single mistake they made. They should never have tried to exterminate an entire race."

"Oh?" Martel allowed his voice to rise. "So it's *efficiency* again, is it? The only reason you object to the slaughter of six million people is that it was a mistake in strategy?!?"

"That is past history," Schlimmermann said tightly. "It has nothing to do with the present inquiry."

"It has everything to do with it—if it helps explain why you decided to play God. You killed three thousand people, Ambassador. Why? To prove that you could?"

"No!"

No!

Martel: "You're lying again."

Schlimmermann jumped to his feet and glared at Shelby over the tables separating them. "Get her out of here!" he shouted. "Get that bitch out! Get her *out!*"

"So you can lie to us with impunity?" Martel shouted back. "Sit down, Ambassador! Sit down, or I'll have the guards restrain you!" Already two uniformed men had moved away from their stations by one of the doors. Radiating hatred, Schlimmermann slowly lowered himself back into his chair.

Shelby sat open-mouthed with shock. The lawyer to her left edged as far away as he could.

Martel waited for the room to settle down. Then he said, "I want a straight answer, Herr Schlimmermann. Are you in sympathy with the purposes of the original Nazi party?"

Schlimmermann sneered. "The Nazis were fools. They let themselves be led by the nose by a demented leader who didn't know how to use the power he had. They became ingrown, corrupt. They had a chance to pull all Europe together into one powerful state and they failed. Am I in sympathy with their purpose of uniting Europe? Of course I am. So are hundreds of thousands of Europeans. It will happen eventually. Soon, I think."

"Their purpose of *uniting* Europe, Ambassador? Or of conquering it?"

"That is a matter of strategy. Of which you spoke earlier with such contempt."

"Don't fence with me, Herr Schlimmermann. Do you approve of the Nazi attempt to conquer Europe?"

"I do not. Subsequent events proved them unworthy to rule their neighbors. They couldn't even rule themselves. The Nazis have become everybody's favorite whipping boy—a fate they well deserve. Very few people are qualified to rule others. Leadership requires strength of will, determination, self-reliance. The flabby philosophical insistence that every man is equal to every other man has only elevated mediocrities to positions of importance, men afraid to act on their own. Such as you, Ambassador Martel. You can't even ask me a question without first checking with that female freak and her little machine. A true leader would be dependent upon no one but himself. Out of every generation only a very few men are fully qualified to lead. Such leaders do not emerge through the democratic process."

"And would one of those men," Martel asked softly, "happen to be named Heinrich Schlimmermann?"

"Not at all. I told you earlier I consider myself a physician practicing preventive medicine. I am simply trying to clear the way for the emergence of the world's rightful rulers."

Schlimmermann's red aura had never throbbed so strongly as it did then. Shelby pressed the *No* button—but it was wasted. None of the commissioners had signaled her. She looked at them anxiously: every member of the commission was watching Schlimmermann with a mixture of revulsion and fascination, so spellbound by what he was saying that they forgot to check on whether he was lying or not. What to do? This was important—they ought to know about it. But Schlimmermann had his audience at last.

Shelby Kent screwed her courage to the sticking place, stood up, and said in a clear voice that carried across the chamber and through every television set in the world turned on at the time, "Ambassador Schlimmermann is lying. He does consider himself one of the world's rightful rulers."

Every head in the chamber swiveled toward her. But Shelby saw only one face, an Aryan face with the mouth drawn back almost in parody of the death rictus, a face with eyes that moved from her to Martel, back to her, back to Martel. Schlimmermann suddenly screamed: a high soprano cry more startling in its pitch than its un-expectedness. Then the German was climbing over the table in front of him, heading for a point somewhere between Shelby and Martel. *Which one of us is he after?* she thought woodenly, unable to move. *Move*, she told herself, and stood rooted where she was.

Schlimmermann didn't get far. Guards swarmed among the tables, over the tables, over Schlimmermann. His outburst ended abruptly, as if someone had flipped an *off* switch. The German managed to carry himself with dignity and even pride as the guards led him from the hearing chamber. The room buzzed with excitement. Martel was on his feet, ashen-faced. He and Shelby stared at each other for a long moment, neither of them speaking. Then Shelby heard a sound that made her turn her head, a sound incongruous to the other sounds in the room.

It was Li Xijuan. She was laughing.

CHAPTER 37

A HIT, A PALPABLE HIT!

"He's not here," the stage doorkeeper glowed redly.

Shelby cleared her throat.

Max caught it. "Ah, but he is," he told the doorkeeper. "He's inside right now, waiting for me. Check your list again."

The doorkeeper picked up a clipboard. "Bradford?"

"Bradley. Max Bradley."

"I got a Mac Bradford."

"That's me," Max sighed. "Where is he?"

"Out front. Don't cross the stage—they're rehearsing."

"Right." Max led Tee and Shelby past the usual backstage safety hazards to a side door that opened into the auditorium. The man whom Max had come to see was the producer of the last show Max had designed. The show had turned into a surprise hit, and now plans were afoot to send out a tour company. Meaning a traveling version of the original set was needed. Tee had come along just to give her piano a rest, and Shelby had come along because Tee had come along.

The play currently in rehearsal was another of the producer's projects, one Max had nothing to do with. Shelby and Tee slid quietly into seats on the side aisle as Max made his way over to where the producer was sitting, glaring at the stage like some disapproving Zeus thinking of coming down from Mount Olympus. A fidgety man was pacing the aisles—the director, no doubt. The sisters watched the rehearsal while Max and the producer talked business.

After a while Tee whispered, "What's this play about?"

"I'm not sure," Shelby whispered back. "I think the tall woman is trying to talk the short woman into marrying her husband."

"Whose husband?"

"The tall woman's."

"Bigamy?"

"It's a bit confusing," Shelby admitted.

"Who's the man? The husband?"

"No, he's her brother."

"The tall woman's?"

"The short one's."

"*DON'T WHISPER!*" a voice boomed at them from the stage. "Whispers carry in a theater. If you have to talk, just talk low."

"Yes, ma'am," Tee whispered.

Not too long after that a break was called and everyone could speak in normal tones again. "By the way, I forgot to ask," said Shelby. "What happened in Philadelphia? The show with the two hundred lawn mowers?"

"A bust," Tee sighed. "By the time Max got there the producer had decided to turn the whole thing into a parody of *My Fair Lady*. So Max just got on the next plane and came back home."

Shelby was speechless.

Tee laughed. "Ridiculous, isn't it? From lawn mowers to Cecil Beaton in one easy jump. But it was the word *parody* that did it. Max hates parody. He says anybody can mock—it's what people fall back on when they have no ideas of their own."

By now Max and the producer were standing up, facing each other, nodding their heads vigorously, both talking at the same time. "That means they're almost finished, when they reach that stage," Tee told Shelby.

Sure enough, Max turned up the aisle and gestured to them to follow. On the street, he said only one word—"Food"—and headed for the nearest eatery. Only when they were seated and had ordered did Max explain to Shelby. "It's that man. I'm always hungry after I've talked to him. He doesn't exactly leave you feeling warm and loved."

Tee was nodding. "He feeds off other people. An awful man."

Max agreed. "A successful producer, but an awful man. Loves his power. Like your buddy Schlimmermann."

"Don't mention him," Shelby shuddered. "I've had enough of that man to last me the rest of my life."

"Haven't we all," Max said.

"Weren't you afraid, Shelby?" Tee asked. "When he started climbing up on the table like that?"

"Damned right I was. I didn't know what he was going to do."

"Did you see any kind of aura around him?" Max asked.

"Nope. Not a thing. Could be he was giving off *something*—maybe that yellow aura Dr. Wedner thinks will come next. But I couldn't see it."

The food arrived and they were all quiet awhile, taking the edge off their hunger. Then Max asked, "What's Kevin Gilbert doing? We haven't seen him lately."

"He's out of town," Shelby said. "On some ultrasecret mission he couldn't tell me about. I don't even know where he's gone."

"Do you miss him?" Tee asked.

"I don't even shoot at him," Shelby said flippantly, and then understood what her sister was really asking her. "Tee, you aren't cooking up some sort of romantic notion about Kevin and me, are you?"

Tee grinned sheepishly. "Is that so awful?"

"Well, not awful maybe. But way off base."

"Why? Now that Eric's gone—"

"Now that Eric's gone, I'm supposed to rebound into the arms of the nearest passing male? Yeah, I saw those movies. I know what's supposed to happen."

"But—"

"Marriage kaput, woman suffers deeply, man simply turns his back and walks away. Woman's only possible release from suffering comes through Meaningful Relationship with new man. Only then can she Find Herself. Get it all together. Get her head on straight. Learn to feel good about herself. Be the real me, her, she, choose one." Shelby sighed. "I think I'll pass."

"Whoa, Shelby, you aren't following the script at all," Max teased. "You didn't even bother with the suffering part. Come on, you can suffer a *little*, can't you? Just to make the story work?"

"Maybe later. Kevin's an attractive man and I enjoy his company —but to burden him with Making Her Life Worthwhile? Not only shallow but presumptuous. No, thanks."

"Aw, Shelby. Everyone should have a partner," Tee said bluely.

"Tee, you're glowing," said Shelby. "And there's no need for it. Really. If I decide I want another partner, I'll go looking for one. But not right now. So stop worrying, please."

Tee sighed deeply. "I like Kevin too—but to tell you the truth, all along I've kinda been hoping you and Eric would get back together."

"Forget about that—it won't happen. The problem between us will always be there. And this new aura I can see now wouldn't help matters any. No, it's best that Eric and I stay on opposite coastlines."

"Pastels are cheaper," Tee muttered.

"Tee, don't worry! Please. There's no need. I prefer it this way." Under Shelby's repeated assurances, Tee's blue aura gradually began to fade.

By the time they were ready to leave and Max was resorting to all sorts of stratagems to attract the waiter's attention, Tee was back to her usual cheerful self. "You don't know how good it is," she told Shelby, "not to have to take that cab ride downtown every day. No more tinkle, tinkle, plonk, plonk. What a relief." Tee had quit her job with Metropolitan Ballet, now devoting all her time to preparing for her upcoming appearance with the Boston Symphony. "I feel good about it, Shel. Better than I've felt about anything I've done in the past three or four years, except marrying Max. I'm going to be ready. I know it."

"Oh, Tee," Shelby smiled, "I've waited a long time to hear that! You don't know how happy you've made *me*. I'm proud of you."

The waiter finally deigned to notice Max and gestured he'd bring their bill sometime in the near future. "Where now?" Max asked.

"Home for me," Tee said, flexing her fingers. "Prokofieff calls."

"Same here," said Shelby. "Did I tell you I'm driving down to New Brunswick later this afternoon?"

"Yes," said Tee.

"No," said Max. "Tests for the blue aura?"

"Pre-testing tests. Tests to help determine the best kind of testing procedures to use. Dr. Wedner wants to start out by investigating the possibility that this blue aura is caused by an excess of beta endorphin in the brain."

"Whazzat?"

"Some kind of drug the brain manufactures. A morphine-like peptide, comes from the pituitary gland. It was Ambassador Aguirrez who made Dr. Wedner think of it—his going into a catatonic state, I mean. Laboratory animals turn catatonic when they're injected with beta endorphin. So maybe the blue aura is caused by a surge in the production of the drug."

"What would cause the surge?" Tee asked.

Shelby lifted her shoulders. "Anxiety, guilt—I don't know, I'm just guessing. That's a whole different ball game, one that requires its own separate testing procedures. What Dr. Wedner wants to do now is establish *that* the blue aura is caused by a drug in the brain, not why. Why will come later."

"I have a feeling," Max said, "that hospitals are going to take the place of police stations in your life."

"That's another thing," Shelby said. "If these tests do prove out, maybe that means the red aura is caused by a peptide too, a different one. You know, up to now Dr. Wedner has been concentrating on *me,* on trying to find out what there is in my physiological makeup that makes me a receptor to these auras. Now he's going to go at it from the other direction—trying to find out why people glow in the first place."

The waiter slapped their bill on the table. "Where," Max asked as they got up to go, "is Dr. Wedner going to get his catatonics for this new testing?"

"Haven't the foggiest. We're nowhere near that stage anyway. He just has some sort of preliminary setup he wants to check out now. I'll be back tomorrow afternoon."

"Well, drive carefully."

"I always do."

CHAPTER 38

THE DRAGON LADY
FLIES AGAIN

It is in the theatre that one gets one's best understanding of their incredibly oversimplified life. A kind of [primitive] view of life where good is good and bad is bad and everything is educational. The latest popular song which we heard everywhere is entitled 'the glow of the declarations of the 10th party congress shines in the heart of the masses like ten thousand stars.' Can you imagine our young whisteling [sic] in their showers 'The latest findings on Watergate disturb the hearts of the people like ten thousand stingy nettles.'

—Marina Sulzberger, in a letter
about China, October 1973

The long table in the United Nations Intelligence Agency conference room could seat exactly thirty people, but only three of the chairs were occupied. Sir John Dudley, P. J. Martel, and Kevin Gilbert crowded together at one end.

"You've just returned from China?" Martel said to Kevin.

"Yes, sir."

"Gilbert was there to co-ordinate information," Sir John explained. "I've had forty additional agents in China for the past three weeks. And we've finally got something."

"About Li Xijuan?"

"About Li Xijuan, about the shipments of defective weapons,

about the Chinese. For some time now it's been clear to me we had to look inside China for the key to what's been happening. There's a labyrinthine quality, an avoidance of the direct about all this—those aren't exclusively Chinese traits, of course, but they do suggest the Oriental mind at work. The hard part is trying to understand what we do see." Sir John smiled. "The Oriental processes of ratiocination are not the same as ours."

Martel grunted agreement. "The word *logic* doesn't mean the same thing in the two hemispheres."

"Whenever Westerners talk about the East," Sir John said, "we invariably yield to the need to simplify what strikes us as being unnecessarily complex. And if you'll bear with me, Ambassador, that's exactly what I'm going to do now."

"Go on."

"There's something basic in the Chinese character that's at the root of everything that's been happening," Sir John said. "China has certain fundamental characteristics that always manage to survive transient political thought. One such—a distrust of partnerships. For over two thousand years the Chinese have looked upon alliances as serving only one purpose—the exploitation of the weaker partner. Never once in its long history has China enjoyed a friendship with another nation. Such a friendship as that between Britain and the United States—to the Chinese mind, it's unthinkable, naïve, hypocritical.

"China's entire history is one of flagrant ethnocentrism, which shows up most noticeably in a strong sense of cultural superiority. The Chinese have never looked upon contact with other countries as a meeting between equals. Their long tradition of dynastic hierarchy has taught the Chinese to think of relationships as existing only between superiors and inferiors. And in relationships between China and other countries, it was China, of course, who was the superior. China has always seen it as natural and right to impose its superior will on the nations surrounding it—by force, if necessary.

"The coming of Communism didn't change any of that. That short-lived alliance with the Soviets—it was bound to collapse, it just wasn't in keeping with the Chinese national character. The Communist experiment in molding the mass mind in no way detracted from that sense of national superiority and the historical need to impose China's will upon others. Peking loved to hurl the charge of imperialism at the rest of the world—your country was the favorite target, Gilbert. But it was the pot calling the kettle black. The Chinese urge to empire was still there, every bit as strong as it was during the Han dynasty.

"A united China has always been an expansionist China," Sir John mused, "and Communism gave a surface unity to a country that had lacked even that for years. Remember the state China was in when Mao came to power—the people were poverty-stricken, mostly illiterate, backward. China was in no condition to compete with the rich industrial nations of the West. But the politically weak countries on China's periphery—ah, they were a different matter altogether. So economic necessity as well as the deeply ingrained desire for Chinese sovereignty drove the People's Republic of China to launch a series of little wars, with the disastrous results we all know.

"What we in the West find so hard to understand is that the Chinese feel they have a moral right to take over these countries. Since the beginning of the Republic back in 1912 the Chinese man on the street has had it drummed into him that his country is entitled to all the territory ever included in the vast Manchu Empire. They consider Korea to *belong* to them because their ancestors had once conquered it."

Martel snorted. "International law recognizes no such claim for recovery. A sanction for stealing whole countries? Nonsense."

"To the Chinese it makes perfect sense," said Sir John. "They lay claim to all lands ever invaded by Chinese armies in the past. Thailand, Laos, Vietnam, Cambodia, most of Burma—all former vassals of the Empire. It came clear in the sixties where they were heading. If they could push on south to the Indonesian island countries, they'd control a vast section of the world's shipping industry. They have other claims as well—some of them based on ethnological links or other matters that placed little countries like Bhutan and Sikkim within the Chinese 'sphere of influence.' And Nepal—putting China in India's back yard. If the Chinese ever feel strong enough to challenge Soviet Russia, they'll undoubtedly start by claiming Mongolia and Western Turkestan on the same grounds." Sir John paused. "And that, we have found out, has become a viable possibility in the past few years."

Martel didn't look particularly impressed. "War between China and Russia—I'm sorry, Sir John, but that's not exactly a new bogeyman. One of Li Xijuan's strongest arguments in favor of establishing an international militia was that it could police borders separating unfriendly nations. She used her own country and the Soviet Union as an example, I remember."

"Exactly!" Sir John said triumphantly. "That's the key. I'm going to let Gilbert tell you the rest."

"It's been a very confusing experience for me," Kevin Gilbert said. "Our agents in China gave me so many conflicting reports that it was a while before I understood they were *all* accurate. Feudalism in one part of the country and agrarian communism in another. Fascism hiding behind the slogans of Marx and Mao existing side by side with a free speech movement sponsored by writers and artists. The enormous complexity of this country is something that just can't be taken in all at once. Sir John spoke of a 'surface' unity Communism imposed on China—that's exactly what it was. And just beneath that surface was the bitterest kind of factionalism. Different political sects and sub-sects and sub-sub-sects warring against each other, literally warring, people sometimes dying in the tens of thousands. Mao couldn't control it. At times he'd side with one faction or another, but mostly he just ignored them all—hoping they'd kill each other off, no doubt."

"Then it's true?" Martel asked. "I've heard those stories, of course, but one never knows what to believe of the news coming out of China."

"Yes, that was the trouble. Communist newspapers never reported 'negative' news, and it's only recently that the Chinese have been willing to talk about what was going on. Then in 1976 Mao died— that started the change. All these conflicting factions began to come out into the open. The country's intellectuals came back from the pig farms or wherever they'd been sent for punishment, and certain daring souls began voicing the opinion that maybe democracy wasn't so bad after all. Then came the eighties and Mao himself was discredited, inevitably.

"The Chinese are a strange people—they turn on each other at the drop of a hat. They present a more-or-less unified front to the rest of the world, but they treat each other abominably. For instance, you can find the traditional scorn for peasants in even the most educated of the people. The peasants are invariably greeted with curses and blows—just for being peasants. And if a peasant should ever rise to a position of some political authority, he turns right around and exploits his fellow peasants the same way he himself had earlier been exploited. Building a little empire for himself, you see. The enforced equality of Communism simply didn't take. That's why the reaction against Mao, when it came, was so very strong. But even while they were flirting with the idea of democracy, the Chinese were still thinking in terms of superior–inferior relationships, still xenophobic. Mao was discredited, but the power structure he left behind still functioned—in a way. It too had splintered, into a hundred different factions—"

"A hundred?" said Martel, incredulous.

"Conservative estimate," Kevin said. "It's hard to be accurate because the factions themselves are still in a constant state of flux. Some have died, some united with others, some split into sub-factions. But on one point there was no disagreement. The Chinese encroachment of neighboring lands continued. What Sir John called China's urge to empire wasn't weakened by the political infighting. The Chinese disagreed about *how*, not about *what*.

"One of the Communist sub-sects gradually grew more powerful than its rivals, retaining control of the Army and therefore of the country. It was this faction that appointed Li Xijuan Ambassador to the UN. And it was this faction that got tired of piddling around in Cambodia and Thailand and decided to go after bigger game. Mongolia, in fact. Sir, do you remember when Li Xijuan was recalled to China?"

"Yes, I do," Martel said. "It came at an awkward time—she was right in the middle of the organizational work her Militia Committee was doing."

"And that's why she was recalled—the Militia. She was instructed to sabotage the project."

Martel grunted.

"Her party didn't want UN Militiamen standing between them and Mongolia. One of our agents located a man who'd been a member of the inner circle that made that decision. The man is now *persona non grata* and spends his days repairing farm tractors, but he can still talk. He said he was convinced Li Xijuan was opposed to an invasion of Mongolia, but she never came right out and said so. Instead, what she did was convince her superiors that a UN Militia could be *used* by the Chinese, that if the Russians could be enticed into attacking first the Militia would do their fighting for them. Finally the party agreed and sent her back to New York to finish her work."

"I don't quite follow," Martel said. "How would providing defective weapons to isolated groups of insurgents provoke the Russians into attacking China?"

"It wouldn't. Li Xijuan had no such instructions from home—she was acting strictly on her own. Our discredited informant was right. Li Xijuan thought an invasion of Mongolia would be a mistake—*at this time*. The country is still too divided, still too far behind technologically, still not strong enough to take on the Russian giant. Li Xijuan's problem was to find a way of convincing the party leaders that the time was not yet ripe for further expansion."

"So arming the insurgents—"

"Was nothing more than a goddamned object lesson. Li Xijuan didn't give a hoot about stage-managing controlled rebellions. What she wanted was the *inquiry*—a public, televised demonstration of authority so strong that even the most invasion-hungry of her compatriots would think twice about proceeding. Sir John spotted it—he said it was the publicity she was after. Her idea for using the Militia to fight the Russians—that was just a stall. She must have seen this invasion plan coming for a long time—that's probably why she worked so hard to get the Militia established. A true world army was inevitable. Li Xijuan just hurried it along a little, seeing it as a political reality that would have to be dealt with and one which could possibly be turned to her own advantage."

"And Aguirrez and Schlimmermann?"

"Convenient villains. Li Xijuan must have felt she was running out of time and needed some help to provoke an inquiry. Aguirrez was malleable, and Schlimmermann—well, Li Xijuan knew Schlimmermann felt his 'superiority' had remained hidden too long. His resentment had been building up for years—he wouldn't be able to resist the temptation to power. That unearned sense of importance was just about due to bust loose."

"Schlimmermann's a throwback," Sir John interposed, "the kind of German who's an embarrassment to his countrymen. They still think about Hitler, you know. They think about him a lot. Even people who hadn't been born yet when the Nazi ulcer was festering. They know what they're capable of, and it scares them. A Schlimmermann is what they want *not* to happen."

"I just had a horrible thought," said Martel. "We know Li Xijuan approached other ambassadors before she hooked these two fish. I'm not sure I want to think about her first choice—the one she wanted *before* Schlimmermann."

Kevin Gilbert said, "Maybe we'd be better off if she'd gotten her first choice. I'd guess she'd go for someone more manageable than Schlimmermann. Aguirrez turned out to be a good choice—he was very active. Schlimmermann almost queered the deal for her. He killed the wrong people. Li Xijuan probably felt like strangling him when he refused to follow her scenario. But in the end it turned out all right—she got the publicity she wanted. She must have been delighted when she learned we had a human lie detector on our side. Her countrymen could watch her lie to the commission and then watch the commission catch her in her lies. All helping to create an overall impression that the UN could no longer be taken lightly. That's why she supplied the insurgents with faulty weapons—she didn't want to run the risk that they might succeed even temporarily. That would defeat her purpose of demonstrating the UN's strength. And what's the reason for it all? What it all boils down to is that over five thousand people have died just to keep one political party in China from making a tactical error."

All three men were silent for a moment. Then: "Good God," Martel rumbled, "the deviousness of that woman's mind!"

Sir John smiled sadly. "A bit overwhelming, what?"

"Who would ever think of using the *United Nations* as a weapon in an internecine political squabble?!? What gall! Li Xijuan makes Heinrich Schlimmermann's power lust look like nursery play. And her willingness to display herself as a mass murderer before the world?" Martel shook his big head in wonder.

"What the rest of the world thinks doesn't matter," Sir John said. "Superior–inferior, remember. We're the inferior." A phone on a sideboard buzzed softly; Sir John walked over and took the call.

"I'm a little slow," Martel said to Kevin. "Did her plan succeed?"

"We think so," Kevin answered. "There's been no movement of Chinese troops north. We alerted Militia HQ, of course, and our own troops and equipment on the Mongolian border are being reinforced right now. One way or the other, Li Xijuan is getting what she wants. There'll be no invasion of Mongolia this year."

"Puts us in a peculiar position, doesn't it?" Martel grumbled. "The woman stopped a war—or at least postponed it for a while. But at what cost! The casual sacrifice of the lives of five thousand people in no way involved with China's political infighting—it's inexcusable. I must inform the other members of the commission. We'll have some hard questions for Li Xijuan tomorrow—"

"I'm afraid you won't get to ask them," Sir John said dourly as he put down the phone receiver. "Li Xijuan and Schlimmermann have both disappeared."

Martel looked stunned. "Disappeared? You mean they've escaped?"

"Nothing to escape from—they weren't even under house arrest. Their diplomatic immunity can't be revoked because they're being investigated. All we could legally do is place them under 'diplomatic restraints'—which means we ask them not to leave New York. We can't enforce the request. Their residences have been under surveillance, of course, but not guarded. They could just walk out the front door at any time and we couldn't stop them. Even now we have no authority to make an arrest." Sir John looked hard at Martel. "Not unless a criminal charge is brought against them by an authorized agency or commission of the United Nations."

Martel nodded, once. "We'll vote on an indictment as soon as I can call the commission together," he promised grimly.

"In that case, Ambassador, you'll excuse us? We have no time to lose."

CHAPTER 39

LORD HELP THE MISTER

(*who comes between me and my sister*)

Where Tee's apartment door had six locks on it, Shelby's had only four. Each sister had keys to the other's apartment, which neither had ever used—until now. It took Tee a while to discover which key fit which lock, but eventually she got her sister's door open. So when Shelby returned from New Brunswick, it was to find a blue-glowing Tee waiting inside for her.

"Oh, Shelby, I was so worried! I can't get in touch with Max and I don't know where Kevin Gilbert is and the police won't help and Dr. Wedner said you'd already left and—"

"Wait a minute, wait a minute—what's wrong?"

"Schlimmermann's escaped!"

"Escaped?"

"Disappeared, the news said. Li Xijuan too, but that doesn't matter because she's not mad at you but Schlimmermann is and—"

"And you think he's coming after me?"

"Well, he might." Tee's voice rose shrilly. "He's a crazy man, Shelby, and he hates you and—"

"Oh, I don't think there's any real danger," Shelby said, nevertheless turning back to check the locks. "Take it easy, Tee. Tell me exactly what happened."

"I don't know what happened." Tee sank down disconsolately on the sofa. "There was a news bulletin on the radio. All it said was that Schlimmermann and Li Xijuan had violated their 'diplomatic restraints'—whatever that means. They've disappeared, and the New

York police are helping UN Intelligence look for them. That's all I know."

Shelby sat on the sofa arm and thought this over. "If they've both decided to make a run for it, they're probably trying to get as far away from New York as they can. I don't think Schlimmermann would hang around here just for a chance of getting back at me."

"Shelby, you know he's not rational! He thinks he can do anything —the man thinks he's God. He could very well want to 'punish' you before he . . . before he goes on and does whatever it is he wants to go on and do."

In spite of herself, Shelby shivered. "You said you called the police?"

Tee made a face. "They say they can't spare anyone to stand guard. They don't seem to think you're in any real danger."

"Well, I don't either," Shelby said briskly, putting a decisiveness into her voice she didn't really feel. She flipped on the television. "Watch to see if there are any more announcements. I've got to take a shower—I feel grungy. There's nothing on this time of day but reruns—they'll interrupt if there's any news."

Tee nodded listlessly and stared at the screen. Once in the shower Shelby decided to wash her hair as well. Ten minutes ago she hadn't felt in any particular need of cleansing, but the news about Schlimmermann had made her feel dirty. Hot water and lots of suds—that would help.

She pulled on an old terry cloth robe Eric had left behind and went out to find Tee sitting hypnotized on the edge of the sofa. "What's so fascinating?"

"Oh, just Mr. Spock leaning in a doorway," Tee said without looking away from the screen. "Grinning from ear to ear for all the world like an overgrown elf."

"Grinning? I thought he never even smiled."

"It's not really Mr. Spock who's grinning, just his face," Tee explained. "There's somebody else inside his body."

"Oh sure, I should have figured that out for myself." Shelby stood behind the sofa toweling her hair, looking over Tee's head at the television set. The enmity between Mr. Spock-Who-Was-Not-Mr. Spock and Captain Kirk-Who-Was-Not-Captain Kirk was coming out into the open. *Be careful! Danger!*
CCRRAA-AA-AA-ACCKK!

The sound made both Shelby and Tee jump. "What is it?" Tee cried.

CRA-A-A-ACK! it came again. Both women swiveled toward the door and saw the end of a crowbar poking through between the door and the frame, splintering the wood of both the door and the jamb. *Eric always said we should have a steel door put in,* was all Shelby could think.

Now the crowbar was hacking away at the door, knocking pieces of splintered wood to the floor. Shelby stood frozen at the sight of the crowbar penetrating her defenses, its phallic invasion of her space making her numb with fear. It was the sound of Tee whimpering that brought Shelby out of her trance. She made a dive for the phone and managed to dial 911 before what was left of the door gave way.

Heinrich Schlimmermann stepped through the doorway. Breathing heavily from his exertions, tense, carrying more hatred than he knew what to do with. He saw Shelby at the phone—and without stopping to think, heaved the crowbar at her.

She almost got out of the way. The crowbar hit only a glancing blow against the side of her head, but it was enough. Shelby dropped like a ton of bricks. As she went down she was vaguely aware of someone SCREAMING, *screaming,* screaming . . .

. . . screaming, *screaming,* SCREAMING! The tickle of carpet dust in her nostrils brought her back to consciousness. *Rug needs shampooing,* she thought dully. Who's that screaming . . . Tee? Is that Tee? *Schlimmermann! What's he doing to Tee?*

Painfully she lifted her head and tried to see what was happening. She could barely make out two fuzzy figures with their arms wrapped around each other. Almost an embrace—no, it *was* an embrace. What was Schlimmermann doing to Tee? Why were they embracing? Shelby made a desperate effort to focus her eyes and saw it wasn't Schlimmermann and Tee at all—it was Captain Kirk kissing a woman member of his crew. The screaming was coming from another part of the room.

Shelby pulled herself up to her knees, aware for the first time that the front of her robe was covered with blood. She started to crawl in the direction of the screaming. And then she saw.

Tee had her hands locked into Schlimmermann's neck, her steel fingers digging into his throat. Schlimmermann was beating at her with his hands and arms and kicking at her. Every time a blow landed, Tee screamed. But she held on.

A wave of dizziness swept over Shelby. She fought down a need to vomit and forced herself to go on with her crawl toward Tee and Schlimmermann. When next she looked the German was down on his knees, his eyes and mouth wide, his hands pulling at Tee's arms. But his movements were weak, ineffectual. Tee kept screaming, screaming.

By the time Shelby reached her sister, Schlimmermann's arms were hanging limply at his sides. Tee's eyes were glazed, seeing nothing, her hands like a vise around the German's neck. And still she screamed.

Shelby used a chair to pull herself to her feet and shouted to make herself heard over her sister's screams. "Tee, let go! It's all over! You can let go now! Tee, *look at his face!*"

Tee turned her glazed eyes toward Shelby and gradually brought them back into focus. Then she looked at Schlimmermann.

His face had turned blue.

Tee unlocked her hands and let Schlimmermann fall away from her. The two sisters stood huddled together, their arms around each other, staring at the dead man on the floor.

"Ahead warp factor one," said Captain Kirk.

CHAPTER 40

TAKE TWO ASPIRINS

Sic transit gloria mundi.
(On Monday Gloria threw up in the subway.)

This too shall pass.

Already the horrors of yesterday were beginning to dim. Shelby and Tee were beginning to see and feel and think normally again, awed by what had happened and grateful to find they were both still alive.

They'd still been holding on to each other by Schlimmermann's body when the police stepped through the shattered doorway—followed immediately by Kevin Gilbert. Kevin had taken in the scene in one glance and moved into action. He flashed his ID at the officer in charge, put one arm around each of the sisters, and swooped them both off to a hospital before anyone could think *Call an ambulance.*

The hospital was a scene of confusion for Shelby—strange voices, bright lights, funny smells. Fingers poking at her. Once, flat on her back, she looked up to see a white-faced Max peering down at her. "Tee?" she asked him.

"She's all right," Max had time to say before someone told him to leave.

Shelby didn't notice she'd lost her bloody robe and was wearing a hospital gown until they were taking stitches in her scalp. "Only four stitches," a voice reassured her. "It's not bad at all. But we want to keep you here overnight for observation."

Tee had quite a few cuts and bruises where Schlimmermann had hit and kicked at her. But she was quickly patched up, given a sedative, and sent home with Max. "Do you think the Boston Symphony will still want me after this?" she asked woozily as they left.

"The only thing the Boston Symphony is going to worry about," Max told her, "is whether or not you hurt your hands. Come along now."

The first thing Shelby saw when she opened her eyes the next morning was Kevin Gilbert, sleeping uncomfortably in a chair beside her hospital bed. She sat up in bed carefully, taking inventory. Her head was sore where the stitches had been taken and she needed to go to the bathroom, but everything else seemed to be all right. She fingered the bandage on her head. Kevin opened one eye and looked at her.

"Have you been there all night?" she asked.

"Almost," he yawned. "I went to your place and got you some clothes. I think they'll let you go today if you're feeling okay. Do you know how you feel yet?"

"Pretty good, considering. Do I have a bathroom here?"

"Over there," he pointed.

Shelby was released from the hospital with strict instructions to go straight home to bed. She promised faithfully and then went straight to the police station instead. Kevin said the police wanted a statement.

On the way, she asked how Tee was doing.

"Bearing up beautifully," Kevin said with a note of surprise in his voice. "I talked to Max this morning, and he said she's sore and a little stiff from the pummeling she took, naturally. But she's not in shock or anything like that—she's doing fine. They'll both be at the police station. You can see for yourself."

"That's something I don't understand," Shelby said. "How did the police get there? I remember dialing 911 but I didn't have time to say anything. Who called the police?"

"Your neighbors." Kevin smiled grimly. "Between the two of them, Schlimmermann and Tee made enough noise to wake the dead. Almost everyone in your building called for help."

Something was bothering Kevin; it was the first time Shelby had ever seen him glowing blue. She almost asked him what was wrong but held off.

Inside the police station, Tee came limping toward them followed by Max and a policeman. The sisters touched hands by way of greeting. "Okay?" asked Shelby.

"I feel like an old lady," Tee complained. "How's your head?"

"Hurts, but not as much as it did. What are we supposed to do here?"

"I've just signed my statement. Now you make yours, and then they decide whether to lock me up or not."

Max sighed. "She'll do anything to get out of performing in public."

"Not this time," said Tee. "I, am, going to Boston. Even if you have to spring me out of the joint. Or is it slammer?" She turned to the policeman. "What do you call it?"

"We call it prison," the policeman said.

Shelby made her statement to a police stenographer. Soon after, Tee was officially informed no criminal charges were being brought against her. Both she and Shelby were apprised of the time and place of the inquest and told in no uncertain terms to be there.

Tee let out a big breath she'd been holding. "I was pretending I was sure I wouldn't be charged, but I wasn't sure at all. I was scared."

"You're the bravest scared lady I know," Max said, hugging her.

"Ow!" Tee ow-ed. "Careful of that arm."

Shelby turned to Kevin. "Kevin, how can I ever thank you? For taking charge yesterday, for helping today—"

"Oh Shelby, don't," he said uncomfortably. "Don't thank me. I'm the one who almost got you killed in the first place."

"*You* are?" Shelby and Tee said together.

Max: "You want to explain that?"

"I should have anticipated what Schlimmermann would do," Kevin said. "I should have sent someone over to protect you the minute I heard he'd disappeared. Because I didn't think, you were almost killed."

"I see," said Shelby. "Well now, how does it go? Tee has bumps and bruises, I have a bloody head, and Kevin has opted for guilt feelings. What about you, Max? What are you suffering from?"

"Got a nasty hangnail here," Max said, staring somberly at a forefinger.

"Perfect. Now we've all got something to complain about. But there's a problem. Tee and I have doctors, and I know how to take care of a hangnail. But what do you do for guilt feelings?"

"Chicken soup?" Tee suggested.

Kevin was looking so amazed that the other three burst out laughing.

"I almost got you killed and you make a joke of it?" Kevin couldn't believe it.

"We're making a joke of it because we're still a little scared," Max explained. "It helps. Nobody expected you to second-guess a madman, Kevin. *Tee* guessed, but musicians are all slightly mad themselves."

"Hey," said Tee.

"So don't go blaming yourself because you couldn't read Schlimmermann's mind. Personally, I'd have thought he'd go after P. J. Martel if he went after anybody."

Kevin looked at Shelby.

"Nobody blames you," she said.

"Thank you," he said simply. "Now I think it's time we got you home. You're supposed to get lots of rest for the next few days."

"Do you have your car here?" Max asked Kevin. "Mine's in the garage again."

They all piled into Kevin's car. Shelby watched the stiff way her sister climbed into the back seat and asked, "Are you feeling all right, Tee?"

Tee eased back into the seat and held out her hands, palms down. "Steady as a rock," she said. "All I need now is a long soak in a hot tub."

Kevin looked back at her hands, and wanted to touch them. A musician's hands, hands that had been forced to kill. He wanted to tell her that the men in charge were secretly grateful to her, that Sir John and Martel both had been worried Schlimmermann would plead insanity and get away with it. *Had* the man been insane? They would never know. Kevin said nothing and started the car.

"The walrus has been notified, I suppose," Shelby said.

Kevin knew whom she meant. "Last night. He was horrified—stuttering and swearing and yelling. He's holding a round-the-clock session of the commission right now. They're making out their report to the Security Council and requesting that the inquiry be temporarily suspended but the commission itself be kept active. What with Aguirrez in the booby hatch and Schlimmermann dead and Li Xijuan missing, there's no reason to go on with the hearings. Li Xijuan has been formally indicted, you know."

"Then that's it, isn't it? Why not disband the commission?"

"Aguirrez. If he ever recovers, the commission will have to vote on his indictment."

"Why did they run?" Max asked from the back seat. "Schlimmermann and Li Xijuan."

"We think they all three meant to run right from the start. That's why they were so cool about getting caught—none of them was planning on hanging around for the verdict. But only one of them managed to get away—and Li Xijuan's disappearance is only temporary, I promise you."

"She's headed back to China, isn't she?" Max said.

"That's probably what she planned," Kevin agreed. "But the leadership of Li Xijuan's political party isn't too happy with her at the moment. She must have thought she'd go back as Hero of the Republic, or whatever they're calling themselves these days."

"Why would she think that?" Tee asked. "What's heroic about shipping useless weapons all over the world? Or am I allowed to ask?"

"Sure you are," said Kevin. "It'll all be published in the commission's report. Well, briefly, Li Xijuan stirred up all this trouble just to warn her political party that certain plans for war they were entertaining wouldn't work at this time. She forced them to understand the UN would stop them. But instead of being grateful to her for keeping them from making a bad mistake, the party leaders—not too surprisingly—resent being made to look foolish. Ex-Ambassador Li will not be welcomed back with open arms."

Shelby: "Does she know that?"

"We're not certain. I suspect she does."

"So she could be headed anywhere in the world."

"I'm afraid so."

"What is her political party, anyway?" Tee wanted to know. "I thought China was supposed to be a one-party country."

"Ostensibly, it is. But the Communists are divided in China. Li Xijuan's group is that one faction of the Communist Party currently in power. They're fighting not only other Communist factions but also all the other political organizations that have sprung up since Mao's death."

Shelby's mouth twitched. "So the whole thing was a Commie plot?"

Kevin looked at her sadly.

"I didn't say that," Shelby corrected quickly.

They pulled up in front of the Bradley apartment building; Shelby and Kevin watched as Max and a limping Tee disappeared inside. "I can't get over how calmly she's taking everything," Kevin said.

"Tee will be all right," Shelby said confidently.

"What makes you so sure?"

"No blue aura."

Kevin found a parking place not too far from Shelby's building. On the way up in the elevator he said, "I posted a man outside your apartment. That shattered doorway is an open invitation to thieves."

A man leaning casually against the wall in the hallway straightened up when he saw them coming. Kevin said, "All right, Brostoff, you can go now . . ." And stopped in surprise.

Instead of the gaping hole they both expected, they saw a new steel door, fitted and locked. Even the splintered wooden frame had been replaced by a metal one.

The man named Brostoff handed a set of keys to Shelby. "Compliments of Sir John Dudley," he said.

CHAPTER 41

ROGUE BUTTERFLY

Kevin Gilbert caught a glimpse of his reflection in a store window and was surprised at how haggard he looked. Pinched, gray face with dark circles under the eyes. The beginnings of a stoop: he straightened up and walked more briskly than he really wanted to.

He was tired to the point where it would be difficult to relax. Sir John had put him in charge of the search for Li Xijuan—the first time the old man had entrusted him with such a large-scale operation. Kevin had spent two days and one night setting up the machinery, and he'd been tired when he started. The trip to China had taken a lot out of him.

He wasn't sure how he felt about moving from the field to a desk job. He wanted to make the change, and he didn't want to make the change. *Think about it later, when the fatigue is gone.* Kevin was too tired to trust himself behind the wheel of a car, so he stopped a cab and gave the driver the address of the Bradley apartment. Shelby had said she'd be there for a few hours this evening.

Kevin leaned back in the cab and closed his eyes, thinking about Shelby. Thinking about Tee and Max. He was trying not to feel too grateful to these three likable people, with their wildly divergent talents, who seemed willing to take a glorified policeman into their lives. *Don't count on much and you won't be disappointed.*

They had every reason not to accept him. One of the three, the most important one, had almost died because Kevin Gilbert had drawn her into a dangerous situation and then failed to provide her with protection. What if Shelby had been alone when Schlimmermann broke in? Or what if she'd had a sister who was just like other women, who didn't have hands like steel traps? Timid little Tee—what a paradox she was! Afraid of her own shadow, but still able to find reserves of strength that let her kill when killing was the only way to save her sister's life. Tee was put on this earth to create moments of beauty, but she hadn't hesitated to destroy when Shelby was threatened. Tee Bradley was a woman who had her priorities right.

Kevin paid off the driver and buzzed his way into the building. Shelby opened the apartment door, took one look at the shadows under his eyes, and said, "Your circles have circles."

Kevin found himself the object of concern, mildly fussed over by the three people who could so easily have blamed him for what happened. He collapsed gratefully onto the sofa and accepted a life-enhancing, vigor-restoring, confidence-boosting scotch.

"I'll try to be subtle about this," Max said. "You look like hell."

Kevin laughed. "Thanks. All I need is about eight days' sleep and I'll be my usual charming self again. I haven't been to bed since Monday."

"Monday!" said Tee, wide-eyed. "What have you been doing?"

"Top secret stuff," Shelby cautioned.

"No, nothing like that," said Kevin. "I've been organizing the search for Li Xijuan."

That set them all off, speculating about where Li Xijuan might go, what she might do. The guesses ranged from Chinatown in San Francisco to a "lady monastery" in Tibet (Tee's idea). Max thought Li Xijuan would try to make a comeback, like Napoleon. Shelby was sure she'd go straight to a plastic surgeon and change her appearance completely.

"So maybe we should look for a blonde Li Xijuan?" Kevin grinned, going along.

"You scoff, o tracer of lost persons," Shelby said. "But I'll bet anything that's what she does—just blends into the crowd looking like everybody else."

"Do you really think you can catch her?" Tee asked dubiously.

"I'll catch her," Kevin said. "The world gets a little smaller every day. UN Intelligence has an instant-communications setup that sometimes even I don't believe. Wherever she's spotted, I can have an agent on her trail within two minutes."

"Aren't you afraid you'll end up like whatsisname in *Les Misérables?*" asked Shelby. "Chasing poor old Jean Valjean through the sewers of Paris?"

"Javert," Max offered.

"I'll catch her," Kevin said quietly. "And I won't let her go when I do."

"It doesn't fit, Shel," Max objected. "I can't see anybody thinking 'poor old' Li Xijuan. And in the sewers of Paris? Never. The gardens of Versailles, maybe. Or a castle on top of a mountain in South America. But no sewers, nowhere, nohow."

Kevin looked at him curiously. "Do you *admire* the woman, Max?"

Max looked startled, and then said dryly, "I admire her style. But I'm not one of those who confuse style with substance. I understand what she did."

Kevin grinned. "Sorry."

"A strange woman," said Tee. "I'll never understand people like that."

"I want some coffee," Shelby said abruptly. "Do you have any made, Tee?"

"Yes," said Tee, surprised, "but *my* coffee—"

"Happens to be very good," Shelby said firmly. "Sit still—I'll get it. Anybody else?"

"I'd like some," Kevin said as the Bradleys shook their heads. Shelby went into the kitchen.

"Max." Tee had a peculiar look on her face.

"Mm?"

"Did you notice . . . ?"

"Did I notice what?"

"It's only . . . did you happen to notice a faint pink ring around Shelby just now?"

CHAPTER 42

THAT'S ALL SHE WROTE

THE LIBRARY OF CRIME CLASSICS®

FRED ALLEN
Treadmill to Oblivion

CHARLOTTE ARMSTRONG
The Balloon Man
The Chocolate Cobweb
A Dram of Poison
Lemon in the Basket
A Little Less Than Kind
Mischief
The Unsuspected
The Witch's House

JACQUELINE BABBIN
Bloody Soaps
Bloody Special

GEORGE BAXT
The Affair at Royalties
The Alfred Hitchcock Murder Case
The Dorothy Parker Murder Case
I! Said the Demon
The Neon Graveyard
A Parade of Cockeyed Creatures
A Queer Kind of Death
Satan Is a Woman
Swing Low Sweet Harriet
The Talullah Bankhead Murder Case
Topsy and Evil
Who's Next?

KYRIL BONFIGLIOLI
Don't Point That Thing At Me
Something Nasty in the Woodshed

ANTHONY BOUCHER
Nine Times Nine
Rocket to the Morgue

CARYL BRAHMS & S.J. SIMON
A Bullet in the Ballet
Murder a la Stroganoff
Six Curtains for Stroganova

CHRISTIANNA BRAND
Cat and Mouse

MAX BRAND
The Night Flower

HERBERT BREAN
The Traces of Brillhart
Wilders Walk Away

JOHN DICKSON CARR
Below Suspicion
The Burning Court
Death Turns the Tables
The Door to Doom
Fell and Foul Play
Hag's Nook
He Who Whispers
The House at Satan's Elbow
Merrivale, March and Murder
The Murder of Sir Edmund Godfrey
The Problem of the Green Capsule
The Sleeping Sphinx
The Three Coffins
Till Death Do Us Part
Writing as Carter Dickson
The Gilded Man
He Wouldn't Kill Patience
The Judas Window

Nine—and Death Makes Ten
The Peacock Feather Murders
The Plague Court Murders
The Punch and Judy Murders
The Reader Is Warned
The Red Widow Murders
The Skeleton In the Clock
The Unicorn Murders
The White Priory Murders

HENRY CECIL
Daughter's In Law
Settled Out of Court

LESLIE CHARTERIS
Angels Of Doom
The First Saint Omnibus
Getaway
Knight Templar
The Last Hero
The Saint in New York

EDMUND CRISPIN
The Case of the Gilded Fly

CARROLL JOHN DALY
Murder from the East

LILLIAN DE LA TORRE
Dr. Sam: Johnson, Detector
The Detections of Dr. Sam: Johnson
The Return of Dr. Sam: Johnson, Detector
The Exploits of Dr. Sam: Johnson, Detector

PETER DICKINSON
Perfect Gallows
The Glass Sided Ants' Nest
The Sinful Stones

PAUL GALLICO
The Abandoned
Love of Seven Dolls
Mrs.'Arris Goes To Paris
Farewell To Sport
Too Many Ghosts
Thomasina

JAMES GOLLIN
Eliza's Galliardo
The Philomel Foundation

DOUGLAS GREENE & ROBERT ADEY
Death Locked In

DASHIELL HAMMETT & ALEX RAYMOND
Secret Agent X-9

A.P. HERBERT
Uncommon Law

REGINALD HILL
A Killing Kindness

RICHARD HULL
The Murder of My Aunt

E. RICHARD JOHNSON
Cage 5 Is Going To Break
Case Load Maximum
Dead Flowers
The God Keepers
The Inside Man
The Judas
Mongo's Back in Town
Silver Street

JONATHAN LATIMER
The Dead Don't Care

Headed for a Hearse
The Lady in the Morgue
Murder In the Madhouse
The Search for My Great Uncle's Head
Red Gardenias
Solomon's Vineyard

VICTORIA LINCOLN
A Private Disgrace
Lizzie Borden by Daylight

MARGARET MILLAR TITLES
An Air That Kills
Ask for Me Tomorrow
Banshee
Beast in View
Beyond This Point Are Monsters
The Cannibal Heart
The Fiend
Fire Will Freeze
How Like An Angel
The Iron Gates
The Listening Walls
Mermaid
The Murder of Miranda
Rose's Last Summer
Spider Webs
A Stranger in My Grave
Vanish In An Instant
Wall of Eyes

BARRY MALZBERG
Underlay

WILLIAM F. NOLAN
Look Out for Space
Space for Hire

WILLIAM O'FARRELL
Repeat Performance

STUART PALMER
The Penguin Pool Murder

STUART PALMER & CRAIG RICE
People VS Withers and Malone

BARBARA PAUL
Liars & Tyrants & People Who Turn Blue

ELLERY QUEEN
Cat of Many Tails
Drury Lane's Last Case
The Ellery Queen Omnibus
The Tragedy of X
The Tragedy of Y
The Tragedy of Z

PATRICK QUENTIN
Black Widow
Puzzle for Players
Puzzle for Puppets
Puzzle for Wantons

S.S. RAFFERTY
Cork of the Colonies
Die Laughing

DAMON RUNYON
Trials and Tribulations

CLAYTON RAWSON
Death from a Top Hat
Footprints on the Ceiling
The Headless Lady
No Coffin for the Corpse

CRAIG RICE
The Corpse Steps Out
8 Faces at 3
The Big Midget Murders
The Right Murder
The Wrong Murder

GEORGE SANDERS
Crime On My Hands

WALTER SATTERTHWAIT
Miss Lizzie

HAKE TALBOT
Rim of the Pit

ROBERT TAYLOR
Fred Allen
His Life and Wit

DARWIN L. TEILHET
The Talking Sparrow Murders

P.G. WODEHOUSE
Full Moon
If I Were You
Plum's Peaches
Service with a Smile
Tales From the Drone's Club
Who's Who In Wodehouse
Wodehouse On Crime